BEFORE THE COFFEE GETS COLD

Also by Toshikazu Kawaguchi

Tales from the cafe
Before your memory fades
Before we say goodbye

Toshikazu Kawaguchi

BEFORE THE COFFEE GETS COLD

Translated from the Japanese by Geoffrey Trousselot

PICADOR

First published 2019 by Picador

This edition first published 2023 by Picador
an imprint of Pan Macmillan
The Smithson, 6 Briset Street, London ECIM 5NR
EU representative: Macmillan Publishers Ireland Ltd, 1st Floor,
The Liffey Trust Centre, 117–126 Sheriff Street Upper,
Dublin 1, DOI YC43
Associated companies throughout the world
www.panmacmillan.com

ISBN 978-1-5290-2958-1

Originally published in Japan as COFFEE GA SAMENAI UCHINI
by Sunmark Publishing Inc., Tokyo, Japan in 2015.
Japanese/English translation rights arranged with Sunmark
Publishing, Inc., through InterRights, Inc., Tokyo, Japan and Gudovitz & Company Literary
Agency, New York, USA

40

A CIP catalogue record for this book is available from the British Library.

Typeset in Giovanni by Jouve (UK), Milton Keynes
Printed and bound by CPI Group (UK) Ltd, Croydon, CRO 4YY

Visit **www.picador.com** to read more about all our books
and to buy them. You will also find features, author interviews and
news of any author events, and you can sign up for e-newsletters
so that you're always first to hear about our new releases.

If you could go back, who would you want to meet?

Relationship map of characters

Woman in the White Dress

A ghost who occupies the seat that returns you to the past. She leaves to use the toilet once a day. Usually she is found quietly reading her novel. But she curses anyone who disturbs her.

Nagare Tokita

Cousin of Kazu Tokita and owner of the cafe. He is a giant of a man, almost two metres tall. He is married to Kei.

Kumi Hirai

Younger sister of Yaeko. She runs the family-owned inn but originally didn't want to. She often comes to Tokyo to persuade Yaeko to return home.

Kei Tokita

Wife of Nagare. She has a weak heart, which means that her pregnancy is very dangerous for her.

travelled to the future

returned to the past

Yaeko Hirai

She runs a nearby snack bar. Her parents disowned her when she left home because she did not want to run the family inn.

Kazu Tokita

Cousin of Nagare Tokita and waitress of the cafe Funiculi Funicula. She serves the coffee during the ceremony that returns people to the past.

returned to the past

returned to the past

Fumiko Kiyokawa

A week ago her boyfriend told her he was going to work in America and they split up.

Ms Kohtake

A nurse and a regular of the cafe. She travels back in time to receive a letter from her husband.

Goro Katada

Fumiko's boyfriend. He has gone to work in America.

Mr Fusagi

He wrote a letter to his wife that he didn't manage to give her. He has early onset Alzheimer's disease and cannot remember who she is.

CONTENTS

I

The Lovers

'Oh gosh, is that the time? Sorry, I have to go,' the man mumbled evasively, as he stood up and reached for his bag.

'Eh?' the woman said.

She glared with uncertainty. She hadn't heard him say it was over. But he had called her – his girlfriend of three years – to come out for a *serious conversation* . . . and now he had suddenly announced he was going to work in America. He was to leave immediately – in a few hours. Even without hearing those words, she knew now that the *serious conversation* was about breaking up. She knew now it was a mistake to have thought – to have hoped – that the *serious conversation* might have included '*Will you marry me?*' for example.

'What?' the man responded dryly. He didn't make eye contact with her.

'Don't I deserve an explanation?' she asked.

The woman spoke using an interrogative tone the man particularly disliked. They were in a windowless basement cafe.

The lighting was provided by just six shaded lamps hanging from the ceiling and a single wall lamp near the entrance. A permanent sepia hue stained the cafe interior. Without a clock, there was no way to tell night and day.

There were three large antique wall clocks in the cafe. The arms of each, however, showed different times. Was this intentional? Or were they just broken? Customers on their first visit never understood why they were like this. Their only option was to check their watches. The man did likewise. While looking at the time on his watch, he started rubbing his fingers above his right eyebrow while his lower lip began to protrude slightly.

The woman found that expression particularly exasperating.

'And why are you looking like that? Like I'm the one being a pain?' she blurted out.

'I'm not thinking that,' he replied sheepishly.

'Yes you are!' she insisted.

With bottom lip again protruding, he evaded her stare and offered no reply.

The man's passive behaviour was infuriating the woman more and more. She scowled. 'You want it to be me who says it?'

She reached for her coffee, from which all heat had now gone. With the sweetest part of the experience lost, it sent her mood plummeting further.

The man looked at his watch again and counted back from the boarding time. He had to leave the cafe very soon. Unable to compose himself any better, his fingers had found their way back to his eyebrow.

The sight of him so obviously hung up about the time annoyed her. She recklessly plunked the cup down on the table. It came down hard on the saucer. *Clang!*

The loud noise startled him. His fingers, which had been busy caressing his right eyebrow, began to pull at his hair. But then, after taking a short deep breath, he sat back down and looked her in the face. All of a sudden, his face was calm.

In fact, the man's face had so clearly changed that the woman was quite taken aback. She looked down and stared at her hands clenched on her lap.

The man who had worried about time didn't wait for the woman to look up. 'Now, look . . .' he started.

No longer muttering, he sounded collected and together.

But as if she was actively trying to stop short his next words, the woman said, 'Why don't you just go?' She didn't look up.

The woman who wanted an explanation now refused to hear it. The man sat motionless as if time itself had stopped.

'It's time for you to go, isn't it?' she said, as petulantly as a child.

He looked at her perplexed, as if he didn't understand what she meant.

As if she was aware of how childish and unpleasant she sounded, she uncomfortably averted her eyes from the man and bit her lip. He rose from his seat, and spoke to the waitress standing behind the counter.

'Excuse me, I'd like to pay,' he said in a small voice.

The man tried to grab the bill, but the woman's hand was pressing down on it.

'I'm going to stay a bit longer . . . *so I'll pay*,' was what she meant to say, but he had pulled out the bill from under her hand with ease and was walking to the cash register.

'Together, thanks.'

'Oh, I said leave it.'

Not moving from her chair, the woman reached out her hand to the man.

But the man refused to look at her. He pulled out a thousand-yen note from his wallet.

'Keep the change,' he said as he handed the waitress the note together with the bill. The man turned his face filled with sadness to the woman for a split second, as he picked up his bag and left.

CLANG-DONG

'. . . and that happened one week ago,' said Fumiko Kiyokawa.

Her upper body flopped into a heap on the table like a deflating balloon. As she collapsed, she somehow avoided spilling the coffee cup in front of her.

The waitress and the customer seated at the counter who had been listening to Fumiko's story looked at each other.

Before Fumiko had finished senior high school, she had already mastered six languages. After graduating top of her class from Waseda University, she joined a major medical-related IT firm in Tokyo. By her second year at the firm, she was already directing numerous projects. She was the epitome of the smart, career-driven woman.

Today, Fumiko was dressed in ordinary business attire: a white blouse and black skirt and jacket. Judging by her appearance, she was on her way home from work.

Fumiko's looks were better than ordinary. Blessed with well-defined features and petite lips, she had the face of a pop idol. Her mid-length black hair shone and crowned her with a glowing halo. Despite her conservative clothes, her exceptional figure was easy to discern. Like a model from a fashion magazine, she was a beautiful woman who would draw anyone's gaze. Yes, she was a woman who combined intelligence and beauty. But whether she realized this was a different matter.

In the past, Fumiko hadn't been one to dwell on such things – she had lived only for her work. Of course, this didn't mean she had never had relationships. It's just that they never had the same allure for her as work. '*My work is my lover*,' she would say. She had turned down approaches from many men, as though flicking away specks of dust.

The man she had been talking about was Goro Katada. Goro was a systems engineer, and like Fumiko, he was employed by a medical company, though it wasn't a major one. He was her boyfriend – he *was* her boyfriend – and three years her junior. They had met two years ago via a client for which they were both doing a project.

One week ago, Goro had asked Fumiko to meet for a 'serious conversation'. She had arrived at the meeting place in an elegant pale-pink dress with a beige spring coat and white pumps, having caught the attention of all the men she had passed on the way there. It was a new look for Fumiko. She was such a workaholic that, before her relationship with Goro, she had owned no other clothes but suits. Suits were what she had worn on dates with Goro as well – after all, they mostly met after work.

Goro had said *serious conversation*, and Fumiko had interpreted this as meaning that the conversation was going to be special. So, filled with expectation, she had bought an outfit especially.

They arrived at their chosen cafe to find a sign on the window saying it was closed due to unforeseen circumstances. Fumiko and Goro were disappointed. The cafe would have been ideal for a serious conversation as each table was in a private booth.

Left with no choice but to find another suitable place, they noticed a small sign down a quiet side street. As it was a basement cafe, they had no way of knowing what it was like inside, but Fumiko was attracted by its name, which came from the lyrics of a song she used to sing as a child, and they agreed to go in.

Fumiko regretted her decision as soon as she peered inside. It was smaller than she had imagined. The cafe had counter and table seats but with just three seats at the counter and three two-seater tables, it only took nine customers to fill the place.

Unless the *serious conversation* currently weighing on Fumiko's mind was to be held in whispers, the entire thing would be overheard. Another negative was the way that everything appeared as in sepia owing to the few shaded lamps . . . it was not to her taste at all.

A place for shady deals . . .

That was Fumiko's first impression of this cafe. She nervously made her way to the only empty table and sat down. There were three other customers and one waitress in the cafe.

At the furthest table sat a woman in a white short-sleeved dress quietly reading a book. At the table closest to the entrance sat a dull-looking man. A travel magazine was spread open on the table and he was jotting memos in a tiny notebook. The woman seated at the counter wore a bright red camisole and green leggings. A sleeveless kimono jacket hung on the back of her chair, and she still had curlers in her hair. She glanced fleetingly at Fumiko, grinning broadly as she did. At several points during Fumiko and Goro's conversation, the woman made a remark to the waitress and let off a raucous laugh.

On hearing Fumiko's explanation, the woman in curlers said, 'I see . . .'

Actually, she didn't *see* at all – she was just following up with the appropriate response. Her name was Yaeko Hirai. One of the cafe regulars, she had just turned thirty and ran a nearby snack, or hostess, bar. She always came in for a cup of coffee before work. Her curlers were in again, but today she was wearing a revealing yellow tube top, a bright red miniskirt and vivid purple leggings. Hirai was sitting cross-legged on the counter chair while listening to Fumiko.

'It was one week ago. You remember, don't you?' Fumiko stood up and directed her attention across the counter to the waitress.

'Hmm . . . yeah,' the waitress answered uneasily, not looking at Fumiko's face.

The waitress's name was Kazu Tokita. Kazu was a cousin of the proprietor. She was waitressing there while attending Tokyo University of the Arts. She had quite a pretty face, a pale complexion and narrow almond-shaped eyes, yet her features were not memorable. It was the type of face that if you glanced at it, closed your eyes and then tried to remember what you saw, nothing would come to mind. In a word, she was inconspicuous. She had no presence. She didn't have many friends either. Not that she worried about it – Kazu was the sort of person who found interpersonal relationships rather tedious.

'So . . . what about him? Where is he now?' Hirai asked, playing with the cup in her hand, not seeming very interested.

'America,' Fumiko said, puffing out her cheeks.

'So your boyfriend chose work, then?' Hirai had a gift for getting to the heart of the matter.

'No, that's not right!' Fumiko protested.

'Eh? But that is right, isn't it? He went to America, didn't he?' Hirai said. She was having a hard time understanding Fumiko.

'Didn't you understand when I explained?' Fumiko said vehemently.

'What bit?'

'I wanted to scream out *don't go* but I was too proud.'

'Not many women would admit that!' Hirai leant back with a snicker, slipped off balance and nearly fell off the chair.

Fumiko ignored Hirai's reaction. 'You understood, right?' she said, looking for support from Kazu.

Kazu feigned a moment's contemplation. 'Basically you're saying you didn't want him to go to America, right?'

Kazu was also one to get straight to the point.

'Well basically, I guess . . . no, I didn't. But . . .'

'You're a difficult one to understand,' Hirai said jovially, after seeing that Fumiko was struggling to reply.

If Hirai had been in Fumiko's place, she would have just broken down in tears. *'Don't go!'* she would have screamed. Of course, they would have been crocodile tears. Tears are a woman's weapon. That was Hirai's philosophy.

Fumiko turned to Kazu at the middle of the counter. Her eyes were glistening. 'Anyway, I want you to transport me back to that day . . . that day one week ago!' she pleaded, totally straight-faced.

Hirai was first to respond to the lunacy of requesting to be sent back to one week ago. 'Back in time, she says . . .' She looked to Kazu with raised eyebrows.

Looking uncomfortable, Kazu simply muttered, 'Oh . . .' and didn't add anything further.

Several years had passed since the cafe had its moment of fame in the light of an urban legend that claimed it could transport people back to the past. Uninterested in that kind of thing, Fumiko had allowed it to fade from her memory. Visiting a week ago was complete happenstance. But last night, she had watched a variety programme on TV. In the introduction, the host spoke about 'urban legends', and like a bolt of lightning striking inside her head, she remembered the cafe. *The cafe that transports you back in time.* It was an incomplete memory, but she remembered that key phrase clearly.

If I return to the past, I might be able to set things right. I might be able to have a conversation with Goro once more. She replayed this fanciful wish over and over in her mind. She became obsessed and lost any ability to make a level-headed judgement.

The next morning she went to work, completely forgetting to eat breakfast. There, her mind was not on the job. She sat

there, obsessed with the passing time. *I just want to make sure.*
She wanted to find out either way as soon as possible – and
not a second later. Her day at work was a long string of careless
mistakes. So sporadic was her attention that a colleague asked
if she was OK. By the end of the day, she had reached peak
scatterbrain.

It took her thirty minutes to get from her company to the
cafe by train. She pretty much ran the last stretch from the station. Entering the cafe feeling quite breathless, she'd walked
up to Kazu.

'Please send me back to the past!' she'd pleaded before
Kazu could even finish saying, *Hello, welcome.*

Her animated gestures had continued in that vein until she
had finished her explanation. But now, looking at the reaction
of the two women, she felt ill at ease.

Hirai just continued to stare at her with a large smirk on
her face, while Kazu wore a deadpan expression and avoided
all eye contact.

If it was true about going back in time, I guess the place
would be thronging with people, Fumiko thought to herself.
But the only people in this cafe were the woman in the white
dress, the man with his travel magazine, and Hirai and Kazu –
the same faces that were here a week ago.

'It's possible to go back, right?' she asked, uneasily.

It may have been prudent to begin with this question. But
it was pointless to realize this now.

'Well, is it or not?' she asked, staring directly at Kazu on the
other side of the counter.

'Hmm. Ah . . .' Kazu replied.

Fumiko's eyes once again lit up. She was not hearing a *no*. An air of excitement started to surround her.

'Please send me back!'

She pleaded so energetically that she seemed about to leap over the counter.

'You want to go back and do what?' asked Hirai coolly, between sips of her tepid coffee.

'I'd make amends.' Her face was serious.

'I see . . .' said Hirai with a shrug.

'Please!' She spoke louder; the word reverberated throughout the cafe.

It was only recently that the idea of marrying Goro had occurred to her. She was turning twenty-eight this year, and she had been interrogated on many occasions by her persistent parents, who lived in Hakodate – *Still not thinking of marriage? Haven't you met any nice men?* and so forth. Her parents' nagging had grown more intense since her twenty-five-year-old sister got married the year before. Now it had reached the point where she was receiving weekly emails. Aside from her younger sister, Fumiko also had a twenty-three-year-old brother. He had married a girl from their home town following a surprise pregnancy, leaving only Fumiko single.

Fumiko felt no rush, but after her little sister got married, her mindset had changed just a little. She had started to think getting married might be OK if it was to Goro.

Hirai plucked a cigarette from her leopard-print pouch.

'Perhaps you'd best explain it to her properly . . . don't you think?' she said in a businesslike manner while lighting it.

'It seems like I should,' Kazu replied in her toneless voice as she walked around the counter and stood before Fumiko.

She looked at her with a soft kindness in her eyes as if she were consoling a crying child.

'Look. I want you to listen, and listen carefully. OK?'

'What?' Fumiko's body tensed up.

'You can go back. It's true . . . you can go back, but . . .'

'But . . . ?'

'When you go back, no matter how hard you try, the present won't change.'

The present won't change. This was something Fumiko was totally unprepared for – something she couldn't take in. 'Eh?' she said loudly without thinking.

Kazu calmly continued explaining. 'Even if you go back to the past and tell your . . . um, boyfriend who went to America how you feel . . .'

'Even if I tell him how I feel?'

'The present won't change.'

'What?' Not wanting to hear, Fumiko desperately covered her ears.

But Kazu casually went on to say the words that she least wanted to hear. 'It won't change the fact that he's gone to America.'

A trembling sensation swept through her entire body.

Yet with what seemed like a ruthless disregard for her feelings, Kazu continued with her explanation.

'Even if you return to the past, reveal your feelings, and ask him not to go, it won't change the present.'

Fumiko reacted impulsively to Kazu's cold hard words. 'That sort of defeats the purpose, don't you think?' she said defiantly.

'Easy now . . . let's not shoot the messenger,' Hirai said. She took a drag of her cigarette, and seemed unsurprised by Fumiko's reaction.

'Why?' Fumiko asked Kazu, her eyes begging for answers.

'Why? I'll tell you why,' Kazu began. 'Because that's the rule.'

There tends to be, in any movie or novel about time travel, some rule saying, *Don't go meddling in anything that is going to change the present.* For example, going back and preventing your parents marrying or meeting would erase the circumstances of your birth and cause your present self to vanish.

This had been the standard state of affairs in most time-travel stories that Fumiko knew, so she believed in the rule: *If you change the past, you do change the present.* On that basis, she wanted to return to the past and have the chance to do it afresh. Alas, it was a dream that was not to be.

She wanted a convincing explanation as to why this unbelievable rule existed, that *there is nothing you can do while in the past that will change the present.* The only explanation that Kazu would give was to say, *Because that's the rule.* Was she trying to tease her in a friendly way, by not telling her the reason? Or was it a difficult concept that she was unable to explain? Or perhaps she didn't understand the reason either, as her casual expression seemed to suggest.

Hirai seemed to be relishing the sight of Fumiko's expression. 'Tough luck,' she said, exhaling a plume of smoke with obvious pleasure.

She had drafted that line earlier when Fumiko had begun her explanation, and had been waiting to deliver it ever since.

'But . . . why?' Fumiko felt the energy drain from her body. As she let herself slouch limply into her chair, a vivid recollection came to her. She had read an article on this cafe in a magazine. The article had the headline 'Uncovering Truth Behind "Time-Travelling Cafe" Made Famous by Urban Legend'. The gist of the article was as follows.

The cafe's name was Funiculi Funicula. It had become famous, with long queues each day, on account of the time-travelling. But it wasn't possible to find anyone who had actually gone back in time, because of the extremely annoying rules that had to be followed. The first rule was: *The only people you can meet while in the past are those who have visited the cafe.* This would usually defeat the purpose of going back. Another rule was: *There is nothing you can do while in the past that will change the present.* The cafe was asked why that rule existed, but their only comment was that they didn't know.

As the author of the article was unable to find anyone who had actually visited the past, whether or not it was actually possible to go back in time remained a mystery. Even supposing it was possible, the sticky point of not being able to change the present certainly made the whole idea seem pointless.

The article concluded by stating that it certainly made an interesting urban legend, but it was difficult to see why the legend existed. As a postscript, the article also mentioned there were apparently other rules that had to be followed but it was unclear what they were.

Fumiko's attention returned to the cafe. Hirai seated herself opposite her at the table she had collapsed onto and proceeded to merrily explain the other rules. With her head and shoulders still sprawled on the table, Fumiko fixed her eyes on the sugar pot, wondering why the cafe didn't use sugar cubes, and quietly listened.

'It's not just those rules. There's only one seat that allows you to go back in time, OK? And, while in the past, you can't move from that seat,' Hirai said. 'What else was there?' she asked Kazu, as she moved her count to her fifth finger.

'There's a time limit,' Kazu said, keeping her eyes on the glass she was wiping. She mentioned it like an afterthought, as if she were merely talking to herself.

Fumiko raised her head in reaction to this news. 'A time limit?'

Kazu showed a slight smile, and nodded.

Hirai gave the table a nudge. 'Frankly, after hearing just these rules, barely anyone still wants to return to the past,' she said, apparently enjoying herself. And she was indeed taking great delight in observing Fumiko. 'It's been a long time since we've seen a customer like you – someone totally set in your delusion of wanting to go back to the past.'

'Hirai . . .' Kazu said sternly.

'Life doesn't get served to you on a plate. Why don't you just give it up?' Hirai blurted out. She looked ready to continue her tirade.

'Hirai . . .' Kazu repeated, this time with a bit more emphasis.

'No. No, I think it's best to clearly put it out there. Huh?' Then Hirai guffawed loudly.

The words spoken were all too much for Fumiko. Her strength had entirely drained from her body, and again she collapsed head and shoulders onto the table.

Then, from across the room . . . 'Can I have a refill, please?' said the man sitting at the table closest to the entrance with his travel magazine opened out in front of him.

'OK,' Kazu called back.

CLANG-DONG

A woman had entered the cafe alone. She was wearing a beige cardigan over a pale aqua shirt-dress and crimson trainers, and carrying a white canvas bag. Her eyes were round and sparkling like a little girl's.

'Hello.' Kazu's voice boomed through the cafe.

'Hi, Kazu.'

'Sis! Hi there!'

Kazu called her sis, but actually she was her cousin's wife, Kei Tokita.

'Looks like the cherry blossoms have had it.' Kei smiled, showing no grief at their passing.

'Yes, the trees are pretty bare now.' Kazu's tone was polite, but not the same polite, civil tone she had used when speaking to Fumiko. Her tone now sounded softer and more like a dove.

'Good evening,' said Hirai as she moved from the seat at Fumiko's table to the counter, appearing to be no longer interested in laughing at Fumiko's misfortune. 'Where have you been?'

'Hospital.'

'What for? Just a routine check-up?'

'Yes.'

'You've got a bit of colour in your face today.'

'Yes, I feel good.'

Glancing over at Fumiko still limp at the table, Kei tilted her head inquisitively. Hirai gave a slight nod, and with that, Kei disappeared into the room behind the counter.

CLANG-DONG

Soon after Kei had disappeared into the back room, a large man poked his head through the doorway, bowing his head to stop it banging into the doorframe. He was wearing a light jacket over his chef's uniform of white shirt and black trousers. A huge bundle of keys was jingling in his right hand. He was Nagare Tokita, the owner of the cafe.

'Good evening,' Kazu greeted him.

Nagare nodded in response and turned his eyes to the man with the magazine at the table closest to the entrance.

Kazu went into the kitchen to bring a refill for the empty coffee cup that Hirai was silently holding up, while Hirai, leaning with one elbow on the counter, quietly observed Nagare.

Nagare was standing in front of the man who was engrossed in his magazine. 'Fusagi,' he said gently.

For a moment, the man called Fusagi didn't react, as if it hadn't registered that his name had been called. Then he looked up slowly at Nagare.

Nagare nodded politely, and said, 'Hello.'

'Oh, hello,' Fusagi said, with a blank expression. He immediately returned to his magazine. For a moment, Nagare continued to stand there looking at him.

'Kazu,' he called to the kitchen.

Kazu poked her face out from the kitchen. 'What is it?'

'Ring Kohtake for me, please.'

The request puzzled Kazu for a while.

'Yes, because she's been looking,' Nagare said, as he turned to face Fusagi.

Kazu understood what he meant. 'Oh . . . Right,' she replied.

After giving Hirai a refill, she disappeared into the back room again to make the phone call.

Nagare cast a sideways glance at Fumiko slumped over the table as he walked behind the counter and took a glass from the shelf. He pulled out a carton of orange juice from the fridge under the counter, poured it nonchalantly into the glass, and gulped it down.

Nagare took the glass into the kitchen to wash it. A moment later, there was the sound of fingernails tapping on the counter.

He poked his head out of the kitchen to see what was happening.

Hirai made a small beckoning gesture. With dripping hands, he approached quietly. She leaned a little over the counter.

'How was it?' she whispered to him as he searched for some kitchen paper.

'Hmm . . .' he mumbled, ambiguously. Maybe it was somehow an answer to the question, or maybe it was just a frustrated grunt while looking for the elusive kitchen paper. Hirai lowered her voice further.

'How were the test results?'

Not replying to this question, Nagare briefly scratched the top of his nose.

'They were bad?' Hirai asked more sombrely.

Nagare's expression did not falter.

'After looking at the results, they decided she doesn't need to be hospitalized,' he explained in a low mumble, almost as if he was talking to himself.

Hirai gave a quiet sigh. 'I see . . .' she said and glanced towards the back room where Kei was.

Kei was born with a weak heart. Throughout her life, she had been in and out of hospital. Nevertheless, having been blessed all her life with a friendly and carefree disposition, she could always manage a smile, no matter how bad her condition got. Hirai was all too familiar with that aspect of her. That was why she checked with Nagare.

Nagare had finally located the kitchen paper and was wiping his hands. 'And how are things with you, Hirai? Are they OK?'

Hirai wasn't sure what Nagare was asking about. Her eyes widened. 'What do you mean?'

'Your sister has been coming to see you a fair bit, hasn't she?'

'Ah. I guess she has,' Hirai answered while she looked around the cafe.

'Your parents run a travellers' inn, right?'

'Yeah, that's right.'

Nagare didn't know about things in much detail, but he had heard that as a result of Hirai having left the family home, her sister had taken over running the inn.

'It must be tough for your sister, alone like that.'

'Nah, she's coping all right. My sister's got the right head for handling that kind of work.'

'But still . . .'

'It's been too long. I can't go home now,' Hirai snapped.

She pulled out a large purse from her leopard-skin pouch. It was so big, it looked more like a dictionary than a purse. Her purse jingled as she began foraging among the coins.

'Why not?'

'Even if I went home, I wouldn't be any help,' she said, tilting her head with a silly smile.

'But . . .'

'Anyway, thanks for the coffee. I have to go,' she said, cutting Nagare short. She put the coffee money on the counter, then got up and walked out of the door, as if she was running away from the conversation.

CLANG-DONG

While picking up the coins that Hirai had left, Nagare glanced at Fumiko slumped on the table. But it was just a glance. He didn't seem very interested in who this woman was, face down on the table. He collected up the coins in his large hands and playfully jangled them.

'Hey, bro.' Kazu's face appeared as she called out. Kazu called Nagare 'bro' despite him being her cousin, not her brother.

'What?'

'Sis is calling you.'

Nagare looked around the cafe. 'OK, coming,' he said. He casually placed the coins in Kazu's hand.

'Kohtake said she'll come straight away,' Kazu said.

Nagare received the news with a nod. 'Look after the cafe, could you?' He disappeared into the back room.

'OK,' she said.

The only people in the cafe, though, were the woman reading a novel, Fumiko, who was slumped over the table, and Fusagi, who was taking notes from the magazine spread open on the table. After depositing the coins in the cash register, Kazu cleared away the coffee cup left by Hirai. One of the cafe's three old wall clocks sounded five deep resonating gongs.

'Coffee, please.'

Fusagi called over to Kazu behind the counter, holding up his coffee cup as he spoke. He had yet to receive the refill he had already asked for.

'Oh . . . right!' exclaimed Kazu, realizing, and hurried back to the kitchen. She came out again holding a transparent glass carafe filled with coffee.

'Even that would be OK,' muttered Fumiko still slumped on the table.

While Kazu was pouring a refill for Fusagi, Fumiko's presence in the corner of her vision attracted her attention.

Fumiko sat upright. 'Even that I can live with. It's OK if nothing changes. Things can stay as they are.' She got up and went over to Kazu, invading her space a little. Gently placing a coffee cup in front of Fusagi, Kazu's brow settled into a frown. She took a couple of steps back.

'Right . . . ah,' she said.

Fumiko drew in even closer. 'So transport me . . . to one week ago!'

It was as if her doubts had been washed away. No longer was there any hint of uncertainty in her speech. If anything, there was just excitement at the chance of returning to the past. Her nostrils were flaring with enthusiasm.

'Um . . . but—'

Becoming uncomfortable with Fumiko's overbearing attitude, Kazu darted around her and moved back behind the counter as if seeking refuge.

'One more important rule,' she began.

In response to these words, Fumiko's eyebrows widened considerably. 'What? There are more rules?'

'You can't meet people who haven't visited this cafe. The present cannot change. There is only one seat that takes you to the past, and you cannot move from it. Then, there is the time limit.' Fumiko counted on her fingers as she ran through each rule, and her anger at them grew.

'This one is probably the most problematic.'

Fumiko was already extremely annoyed with the rules she knew. The news of a further, *most problematic* rule threatened to snap her heart in two. Nevertheless, she bit her lip.

'If that's the case, then fine, so be it. Go on, tell me,' she said, folding her arms and nodding to Kazu, as if to emphasize her resolve.

Kazu drew a short breath as if to say, *I will then*, and vanished into the kitchen, to put away the transparent glass carafe she had been holding.

Left standing there alone, Fumiko took a deep breath to feel more centred. Her initial aim had been to return to the past to somehow stop Goro going to America.

Stopping him from going sounded bad, but if she confessed, *I don't want you to go*, Goro might give up the idea of leaving. If things went well, they might end up never splitting up. At any rate, the initial reason for wanting to go back to the past was *to change the present*.

But if it wasn't possible to change the present, then Goro going to America and them splitting up were also unchangeable. Regardless, Fumiko still yearned passionately to return to the past – all she wanted to do was to go back and see. Her entire objective was centred on the actual act of going back. Her heart was set on experiencing this fantastical phenomenon.

She didn't know whether it was a good thing or a bad thing. *It might be a good thing, and how could it be a bad thing?* she told herself. After she finished a deep breath, Kazu returned. Fumiko's face stiffened like an accused awaiting the court's decision. Kazu stood behind the counter.

'It is only possible to go back in time when seated at a particular seat in this cafe,' she proclaimed. Fumiko reacted instantly.

'Which one? Where should I sit?' She looked around the cafe so rapidly she almost made a whooshing sound as she turned her head from side to side.

Ignoring her reaction, Kazu turned her head and looked fixedly at the woman in the white dress.

Fumiko followed her constant gaze.

'That seat,' Kazu said quietly.

'That one? The one the woman's sitting in?' Fumiko whispered across the counter while keeping her eyes glued on the woman in the dress.

'Yes,' Kazu answered simply.

Yet even before she had finished hearing that short reply, Fumiko was already walking up to the woman in the white dress.

She was a woman who gave the impression that fortune had passed her by. Her white, almost translucent skin contrasted starkly with her long black hair. It may have been spring, but the weather was definitely still chilly on bare skin. Yet the woman was wearing short sleeves, and there was no sign she had a jacket with her. Fumiko was getting the feeling that something was not right. But now was not the time to be concerned with such things.

Fumiko spoke to the woman.

'Er, excuse me, would you mind awfully if we swapped seats?' she asked, holding back her impatience. She thought she had spoken politely and without rudeness; yet the woman in the dress did not react. It was as if she had not even heard her. Fumiko felt a little put out by this. On some rare occasions a person can be so engrossed in a book she does not hear the surrounding voices and sounds. Fumiko assumed that was the case here.

She tried again.

'Hello? . . . Can you hear me?'

'. . .'

'You're wasting your time.'

The voice came unexpectedly from behind Fumiko. It was Kazu. It took her a while to work out what she meant by it.

I only wanted her to give me the seat. Why was I wasting my time? Was I wasting my time asking politely? Wait. Is this another rule? Do I have to clear this other rule first? If that's the case, I think she could say something a bit more helpful than 'You're wasting your time' . . .

Such were the thoughts that were running through her mind. Yet in the end she asked a simple question.

'Why?' she asked Kazu with a look of childlike innocence. Kazu looked directly into her eyes.

'Because that woman . . . is a ghost,' she responded sternly. She sounded deadly serious and like she was telling the absolute truth.

Once again, Fumiko's head was filled with racing thoughts.

Ghost? A real moaning shrieking ghost? The sort that appears under a weeping willow in the summer? The girl just said it so casually – maybe I misheard? But what sounds like 'is a ghost'?

Fumiko's head was awash with many confusing thoughts. 'Ghost?'

'Yes.'

'You're messing with me.'

'No, honestly, she's a ghost.'

Fumiko was bewildered. She was happy not to get stuck on questioning whether or not ghosts actually exist. But what she couldn't accept was the possibility that the woman in the dress was a ghost. She seemed far too real.

'Look, I can clearly . . .'

'See her.' Kazu finished her sentence as if she knew what Fumiko was going to say.

Fumiko was confused. 'But . . .'

Without thinking, she stretched her hand out towards the woman's shoulder. Just as she was about to touch the woman in the dress, Kazu said, 'You can touch her.'

Again, Kazu had a ready reply. Fumiko placed her hand on the woman's shoulder as if to confirm that she could be touched. Without a doubt, she could feel the woman's shoulder and the material of the dress covering her soft skin. She couldn't believe that this was a ghost.

She gently removed her hand. Then once again she placed her hand on the woman's shoulder. She turned to Kazu as if to say, *I can clearly touch her, calling this person a ghost is crazy!*

But Kazu's face remained cool and composed. 'She's a ghost.'

'Really? A ghost?'

Fumiko poked her head towards the woman and looked her squarely in the face, quite rudely.

'Yes,' Kazu replied, with utmost certainty.

'No way. I just can't believe it.'

If Fumiko could see her but was unable to touch her, then she could have accepted it. But this was not the case. She could touch the woman, who had legs. The title of the book the woman was reading was one she had never heard of. It was a normal book, nevertheless – one that you could buy almost anywhere. This led Fumiko to come up with a theory.

You can't really go back to the past. This cafe can't really take you back to the past. It is all just a ploy to get people to come. Take the countless number of annoying rules, for example. These are just the first hurdle to encourage customers wanting to return to the past to give up. If the customer passes that first hurdle, then this must be the second hurdle for those customers who still want to go back in time. They mention a ghost to frighten the person into giving up on the idea. The woman in the dress is just for show. She's pretending to be a ghost.

Fumiko was beginning to feel quite stubborn.

If it's all a lie, then so be it. But I'm not going to be fooled by this lie.

Fumiko addressed the woman in the dress politely. 'Look, it will only be for a short while. Please would you kindly allow me to sit there.'

But it was as if her words hadn't reached the woman's ears. She continued reading without the slightest reaction.

Being totally ignored like this darkened Fumiko's mood. She grabbed the woman's upper arm.

'Stop! You mustn't do that!' warned Kazu loudly.

'Hey! Just stop it! Stop just ignoring me!'

Fumiko tried to forcefully drag the woman in the dress from her seat.

And then it happened . . . The woman in the dress's eyes widened and she glared at her fiercely.

She felt as if the weight of her body had increased many times over. It felt as if dozens of heavy blankets had fallen over her. The light in the cafe dimmed to the brightness of candle-light. An unworldly wailing began to reverberate through the cafe.

She was paralysed. Unable to move a muscle, she dropped to her knees and then fell to a crawling position.

'Ugh! What's happening? What's happening?'

She had absolutely no idea what was happening. Kazu, in a smug, told-you-so kind of way, simply said, 'She cursed you.'

When Fumiko heard *curse*, she didn't understand at first.

'Huh?' she asked with a groan.

Unable to withstand this invisible force that seemed to be getting stronger, Fumiko was now lying face down on the floor.

'What? What is this? What's going on?'

'It's a curse. You went ahead and did what you did, and she cursed you,' said Kazu as she slipped back into the kitchen, leaving Fumiko sprawled on the floor.

Lying face down, Fumiko didn't see Kazu go, but with one ear firmly against the floor, she clearly heard Kazu leave by the sound of her fading footsteps. Her fear was so intense,

Fumiko shivered as if icy water had been poured over her entire body.

'You've got to be kidding. Look at me! What can I do?'

There was no response. Fumiko started shuddering.

The woman in the dress was still glaring at Fumiko with a terrifying expression. She seemed a completely different person to the woman who had been calmly reading her book just moments earlier.

'Help me! Please help me!' Fumiko yelled out to the kitchen.

Kazu calmly returned. Fumiko could not see this, but Kazu was holding a glass carafe of coffee in her hand. Fumiko heard her footsteps coming towards her, but she had no idea what was happening – first the rules, then the ghost, and now the curse. It was all utterly bewildering.

Kazu hadn't even given her any indication whether she meant to help her or not. Fumiko was on the verge of yelling *Help!* at the top of her lungs.

But right at that moment . . .

'Would you care for some more coffee?' Fumiko heard Kazu asking nonchalantly.

Fumiko was incensed. Ignoring her in her moment of need, Kazu was not only *not* helping, she was offering the woman in the dress some more coffee. Fumiko was dumbfounded. *I was clearly told that she was a ghost, and it was wrong of me not to believe it. It was also wrong of me to grab on to the woman's arm and try to forcefully remove her from her chair. But even though I've been yelling 'Help me!' the girl has just been ignoring me and now she is breezily asking that woman if she wants more coffee! Why would a ghost be wanting another coffee!*

'You've got to be kidding!' was all that Fumiko was able to vocalize, however.

But without hesitation, 'Yes, please,' an eerily ethereal voice replied.

It was the woman in the dress who had spoken. Suddenly, Fumiko's body felt lighter.

'Aah . . .'

The curse had been lifted. Fumiko, unencumbered and panting, stood upright on her knees and glared at Kazu.

Kazu returned her gaze, as if to ask, *You have something to say?* and shrugged with indifference. The woman in the dress took a sip from her freshly poured coffee and then returned quietly to her book.

Acting as if nothing out of the ordinary had happened, Kazu disappeared back to the kitchen to return the carafe. Fumiko once more reached her hand out to touch the shoulder of that terrifying woman in the dress. Her fingers could feel her. *The woman is here. She exists.*

Unable to understand such weird events, Fumiko was completely confused. She had experienced the whole thing – she couldn't dispute that. Her body had been pushed down by an invisible force. Though she could not make sense of things in her head, her heart had already fathomed the situation well enough to be pumping gallons of blood through her body.

She stood up and walked towards the counter, feeling quite dizzy. By the time she had made her way there, Kazu had returned from the kitchen.

'Is she really a ghost?' Fumiko asked Kazu.

'Yes,' was Kazu's only reply. She had started topping up the sugar pot with sugar.

So, this totally impossible thing happened . . . Fumiko once more began to hypothesize. *If the ghost . . . and the curse . . . really happened, then what they say about going back in time might also really be true!*

Experiencing the curse had convinced Fumiko that *you can go back.* But there was a problem.

It was that rule – in order to go back to the past, you have to sit in one particular seat. *Sitting in that one particular seat, however, is a ghost. Anything I say doesn't get through to her. And when I tried to sit there forcefully, she cursed me. What am I meant to do?*

'You just have to wait,' Kazu said, as if she could hear Fumiko's thoughts.

'What do you mean?'

'Every day, there is just one moment when she goes to the toilet.'

'A ghost needs to go to the toilet?'

'While she's gone, you can sit there.'

Fumiko stared hard into Kazu's eyes. She gave a small nod. That seemed to be the only solution. As to Fumiko's question of whether ghosts go to the toilet, Kazu was unsure of whether it was genuine curiosity or meant for comedic effect and decided to ignore it with a deadpan expression.

Fumiko drew a deep breath. A moment ago she had been grasping at straws. Now she had a piece of straw in her hand, and she wasn't going to let it go. She once had read a story about a man who traded his way up from one piece of straw to become a millionaire. If she was to become a straw millionaire, she mustn't waste that straw.

'OK . . . I'll wait. I'll wait!'

'Fine, but you should know that she doesn't differentiate between day and night.'

'Yes. OK, I'll wait,' Fumiko said, desperately clutching her straw. 'What time do you close?'

'Regular opening hours are until eight p.m. But if you decide you want to wait, you can wait for as long as it takes.'

'Thank you!'

Fumiko sat down at the middle of the three tables. She sat with her chair facing the woman in the dress. She folded her arms and breathed hard through her nose.

'I'm going to get that seat!' she announced, glaring at the woman in the dress. The woman in the dress was reading her book, as always.

Kazu gave a little sigh.

CLANG-DONG

'Hello. Good evening!' said Kazu, delivering her standard greeting. 'Kohtake!'

Standing in the open doorway was a woman. She looked like she might be a little over forty.

Kohtake was wearing a navy blue cardigan over a nurse's uniform and carrying a plain shoulder bag. Breathing a little heavily as if she had been running, she held her hand on her chest as if to steady her breath.

'Thanks for calling,' she said. She spoke quickly.

Kazu nodded with a smile and disappeared into the kitchen. Kohtake took two or three steps towards the table closest to the entrance and stood next to the man called Fusagi. He didn't seem to notice her at all.

'Fusagi', Kohtake said in a gentle tone that one would normally reserve for a child.

At first, Fusagi showed no reaction, as if he hadn't noticed that she had called him. But noticing her in his peripheral vision, he turned to her with a vacant stare.

'Kohtake', he muttered.

'Yes. It's me', Kohtake said with clear articulation.

'What are you doing here?'

'I had some time off and I thought I might have a cup of coffee.'

'Oh . . . OK', Fusagi said.

He once more cast his eyes down to his magazine. Kohtake, continuing to look at him, sat casually down in the seat opposite. He didn't react to this and instead turned the page of his magazine.

'I hear you've been coming here a lot lately', Kohtake said while studying every nook and cranny of the cafe like a customer who was visiting for the first time.

'Yeah', Fusagi said simply.

'So you've taken a liking to this place?'

'Oh . . . not particularly', he said, in a way that clearly showed that he had indeed taken a liking to the place. A slight smile formed on his lips.

'I'm waiting', he whispered.

'What are you waiting for?'

He turned and looked over at the seat where the woman in the dress was sitting.

'For her to leave that seat', he answered. His face betrayed a boyish glimmer.

Fumiko hadn't particularly been eavesdropping but the

cafe was small. 'What!' she exclaimed in surprise at learning that Fusagi was likewise waiting for the woman in the dress to go to the toilet so he could return to the past.

Hearing Fumiko's voice, Kohtake turned to look at her, but Fusagi paid no attention to her himself.

'Is that so?' Kohtake asked.

'Yeah,' was all that Fusagi said in reply as he took a sip of his coffee.

Fumiko was shaken. *Please don't let me have competition.*

After all . . . she instantly realized that it was her who was at a disadvantage should they both have the same objective. When she had entered the cafe, Fusagi was already there. Since he was here first, it was his turn first. As a matter of common courtesy, she was not going to jump the queue. The woman in the dress only went to the toilet once a day. Therefore there was only one chance to sit in the seat each day.

Fumiko wanted to go back in time right away. She was unable to bear the thought that she might have to wait an extra day, and was unable to hide her agitation at this unexpected development. She leaned sideways and cocked her ear to make sure that Fusagi really did intend to return to the past.

'Did you get to sit there today?' Kohtake asked.

'Not today.'

'Oh, you couldn't sit there?'

'Yeah . . . no.'

Their conversation was doing nothing to allay her worst fears. Fumiko scrunched up her face.

'Fusagi, what do you want to do when you go back in time?'

There was no mistaking – Fusagi was waiting for the woman

in the dress to go to the toilet. This revelation was a huge blow for Fumiko. Disappointment spread across her face and she collapsed onto the table again. The devastating conversation continued.

'Something you want to fix?'

'Ah, well.' Fusagi thought for a moment. 'That's my secret,' he said. He gave a self-satisfied, childish grin.

'Your secret?'

'Yeah.'

Even though Fusagi had said it was a secret, Kohtake smiled as if something was pleasing. Then she looked over to the woman in the dress.

'But it seems like she probably won't be going to the toilet today, does it?'

Fumiko hadn't been expecting to hear that. She reacted automatically, lifting her head from the table. Her movement so swift it was almost audible. *Is it possible that the woman might not even go to the toilet? Kazu said that she goes once a day. But as that woman said, perhaps the woman in the dress has already made today's trip . . . No, that can't be the case. I really hope that's not the case.*

Praying that was not the case, Fumiko waited in trepidation for what Fusagi would say next.

'Perhaps that's right,' he said, readily conceding this point.

No way! Fumiko's mouth opened as if to let out a shriek, but she was dumbfounded by the shock. *Why isn't the woman in the dress going to go to the toilet? What does the woman called Kohtake know?* She was desperate for answers.

Yet she sensed that she shouldn't interrupt the conversation. She had always believed that reading the situation was important, and right now, Kohtake's entire body language was saying, *Stay out of it!* Exactly what she was meant to stay out of was not clear to her. But there was definitely something happening there – and outsiders weren't welcome.

'So . . . how about we leave?' Kohtake said in a gentle, coaxing way. 'Huh?'

Her big chance was back. Setting aside the question of whether the woman in the dress had already gone to the toilet, if Fusagi left, at least she could be rid of her rival.

When Kohtake had suggested that the woman in the dress probably wouldn't be moving today, Fusagi had simply agreed, *Perhaps that's right.* He said *perhaps.* It is equally plausible that he could have meant, *At any rate, I'm waiting to see.* If it was her, Fumiko would definitely wait. She concentrated all of her mental reserves while she waited for his reply, trying not to appear too eager. It was as if her entire body had become her ears.

He glanced over at the woman in the dress, then paused, deep in thought. 'Sure, OK,' he replied.

As it was such a clear and simple reply, Fumiko's heart didn't skip a beat. But even so, her excitement soared and she felt her heart beating fast.

'Right then. We'll leave when you finish your cup,' said Kohtake, looking at the half-empty coffee cup.

Fusagi now seemed to be only thinking about leaving. 'No, it's OK. It's gone cold anyhow,' he said as he clumsily packed away his magazine, notebook, and pencil and got up from his seat.

Putting on his jacket with fleecy sleeves – a type often worn by construction workers – he made his way to the till. With impeccable timing, Kazu came back out of the kitchen. Fusagi passed her the coffee bill.

'What do I owe?' he asked.

Kazu entered the amount using the clunky keys of the ancient cash register. Meanwhile, Fusagi was checking his second bag, his shirt pocket, his back pocket, and every other place he could think . . .

'That's odd, my wallet . . .' he muttered.

It seemed he had come to the cafe without his wallet. After looking in the same places again and again, he still couldn't find it. He looked visibly upset, close to tears, even.

Then Kohtake unexpectedly produced a wallet, and held it in front of him.

'Here.'

It was a well-worn men's leather wallet – folded in half, bulging with what appeared to be a wad of receipts. He paused for moment, staring at the wallet presented before him. He seemed genuinely in a daze. Finally, he took the wallet offered to him without a word.

'How much?' he asked while furrowing into the coin purse as if it was a familiar habit.

Kohtake said nothing. She simply stood behind Fusagi, watching over him as he went about paying. 'Three hundred and eighty yen.'

Fusagi pulled out one coin and handed it to Kazu. 'OK, receiving five hundred yen . . .'

Kazu took the money, entered it into the cash register. Cha-ching . . .

She pulled the change from the drawer.

'That's one hundred and twenty yen change.' Kazu carefully placed the change and receipt in Fusagi's hand.

'Thank you for the coffee,' he said, putting the change

carefully in his wallet. He stowed the wallet in his bag, having seemingly forgotten that Kohtake was there, and he quickly headed for the door.

CLANG-DONG

Kohtake seemed not in the least bothered by his attitude. 'Thank you,' she said simply, and followed on after him.

CLANG-DONG

'They were rather odd,' Fumiko muttered.

Kazu cleared the table where Fusagi had sat and disappeared once more into the kitchen.

The sudden appearance of a rival had upset Fumiko, but now that only she and the woman in the dress remained, she felt sure that victory would be hers.

Right, the competition's gone. Now I just need to wait for her to vacate the seat, she thought. Yet the cafe had no windows and the three wall clocks each showed different times. Without customers coming and going, her sense of time was becoming frozen.

Starting to doze off a little, she reeled off the rules for returning to the past.

The first rule – *the only people one may meet while back in the past are those who have visited the cafe*. Fumiko's parting conversation with Goro just happened to have taken place in this cafe.

The second rule – *no matter how hard one tries while back in the past, one cannot change the present*. In other words, even if

Fumiko returned to that day one week earlier and pleaded for Goro not to go, the fact that he had left for America would not change. She didn't understand why it should be so, and she could feel herself getting upset again thinking about it. But, resigned, she accepted it, given it was the rule.

The third rule – *in order to return to the past, you have to sit in that seat and that seat alone*. This was the seat occupied by the woman in the dress. If you try to sit there by force, you get cursed.

The fourth rule – *while back in the past, you must stay in the seat and never move from it*. In other words, for some reason or other, you couldn't go to the toilet while back in the past.

The fifth rule – *there is a time limit*. Now that she thought about it, Fumiko still hadn't been told the details of this one. She had no idea how long or short this time was. Fumiko thought about these rules over and over. Her thoughts went back and forth. She went from thinking that going back in time was going to be rather pointless to thinking that she may as well take charge of that conversation and say everything she wanted to – after all, it couldn't hurt, could it, if it was not going to change the present? Fumiko went over each rule again and again until finally, slumped on the table, she drifted off to sleep.

The first time Fumiko learned of Goro's dream future was when she dragged him out on their third date. Goro was a gaming geek. He loved those MMORPG (massively multiplayer online role-playing games), which he played on a PC. His uncle was one of the developers of an MMORPG called

Arm of Magic – a game that was popular around the world. Ever since he was a boy, Goro had looked up to his uncle. It was Goro's dream to join the game company his uncle ran: TIP-G. To qualify for the selection exam for TIP-G, it was mandatory to have two things: (1) at least five years' experience working as a systems engineer in the medical industry, and (2) a new unreleased game program that you had personally developed. Human lives depend on the reliability of systems in the medical industry and bugs are not tolerated. In the online gaming industry, on the other hand, people put up with bugs, as it's possible to apply updates even after the release.

TIP-G was different. It only recruited candidates with experience in the medical industry to ensure that only the best programmers were hired. When Goro was telling Fumiko about this, she thought it was a wonderful dream. But what she didn't know was that TIP-G had its headquarters in America.

On their seventh date, Fumiko was waiting for Goro to arrive at their meeting point when a couple of men started talking to her. They were chatting her up. They were good-looking, but she was not interested. Men were always trying to pick her up and so she had developed a technique for dealing with this. Before she could put it to use, Goro arrived and stood there, looking uncomfortable. Fumiko rushed up to him, but the two men reacted, sneered at Goro, and asked her why she was with *that dweeb*. She had no choice but to begin her spiel.

Goro lowered his head and didn't say anything. But she faced the two men and said (in English), 'You guys don't know his appeal,' (in Russian) 'He's brave enough to take on difficult tasks at work,' (in French) 'He has the mental discipline not to give up,' (in Greek) 'He has the skill to render the impossible possible,' (in Italian) 'I also know he has put in extraordinary effort to be able to gain this ability,' (and in Spanish) 'His appeal is far greater than any other man I know.' Then in Japanese, she said, 'If you understood what I just said, I wouldn't mind hanging out with you.'

Visibly stunned, the two men at first stood motionless. Then they looked at each other, and moved on awkwardly.

Fumiko smiled broadly at Goro. 'Naturally, I suppose you understood everything I said,' she said, this time in Portuguese.

Showing his embarrassment, Goro gave a small nod.

On the tenth date, Goro confessed that he had never been in a relationship with a woman before.

'Oh, so I'm the first woman who you've gone out with,' Fumiko said happily. It was the first time she had confirmed that they were actually an item, and Goro's eyes widened at the news.

You could say that night marked the start of their relationship.

Fumiko had been asleep for a while now. Suddenly, the woman in the dress slammed shut the book she was reading and sighed. After pulling out a white handkerchief from her handbag, she slowly stood up, and began walking towards the toilet.

Still asleep, Fumiko hadn't noticed that she had left. Kazu appeared from the back room. She was still wearing her uniform: a white shirt, black bow tie, waistcoat, black trousers, and an apron. While she was clearing the table, she called out to Fumiko.

'Madam. Madam.'

'What? Yes?' Fumiko sat bolt upright in surprise. She blinked her eyes and looked around the cafe until finally she spotted the change.

The woman in the dress was gone. 'Oh!'

'The seat is free now. Do you wish to sit there?'

'Of course I do!' Fumiko said.

She got up in a hurry and walked over to the seat that promised to transport her to the past. It looked like a normal chair, nothing out of the ordinary about it. As she stood there, staring at it with intense desire, her heartbeat quickened. Finally, after getting over all the rules and the curse, she had her ticket to the past.

'OK, now take me back in time by one week.'

Fumiko took a deep breath. She calmed her racing heart and carefully squeezed into the gap between the chair and the table. She had it in her mind that she would travel back to a week ago as soon as her bottom landed on the seat, so her nervousness and excitement were reaching peak levels. She sat down so forcefully, she almost bounced back up again.

'OK. Go back one week!' she exclaimed.

Her heart swelled in anticipation. She looked around the cafe. As there were no windows, there was no way of telling night from day. The three old wall clocks with their hands pointing in different directions didn't tell her the time. But something must have changed. She looked desperately around the cafe, searching for a sign that she had gone back. But she couldn't spot a single difference. If she had returned to a week earlier, Goro would be there – but he wasn't anywhere to be seen . . .

'I haven't gone back, have I?' she muttered. *Don't tell me I've been a fool believing this nonsense about returning to the past.*

Just as she was showing signs of falling apart, Kazu appeared next to her carrying a silver tray, upon which was a silver kettle and a white coffee cup.

'I haven't gone back yet,' Fumiko blurted out.

Kazu's expression was deadpan as always. 'There is one more rule,' she said coolly.

Damn! There was another one. It would take more than simply sitting in the chair.

Fumiko was beginning to get fed up. 'There are still more rules?' she said, yet at the same time, she felt relieved. It meant that going back to the past was still on the cards.

Kazu continued her explanation without showing the slightest interest in how Fumiko was feeling. 'In a moment, I am going to pour you a cup of coffee,' she said as she set a cup in front of Fumiko.

'Coffee? Why coffee?'

'Your time in the past will begin from the time the coffee is poured . . .' Kazu said, ignoring the question from Fumiko, who was nevertheless reassured by the news it would be happening soon. 'And you must return before the coffee goes cold.'

Fumiko's confidence vanished in a flash. 'What? That soon?'

'The last and the most important rule . . .'

The talking never ends. Fumiko was itching to go. 'Too many rules . . .' she muttered as she gripped the coffee cup placed before her. The vessel was quite unremarkable: just a cup which had not yet had coffee poured into it. But she thought it felt noticeably cooler than the usual porcelain.

'Are you listening?' Kazu continued. 'When you return to the past, you must drink the entire cup before the coffee goes cold.'

'Uh. I don't actually like coffee that much.'

Kazu opened her eyes wider and brought her face an inch or so from the tip of Fumiko's nose.

'This is the one rule you have to absolutely obey,' she said in a low voice.

'Really?'

'If you don't, something terrible will happen to you . . .'

'Wh-what?'

Fumiko felt uneasy. It wasn't that she hadn't been expecting something like this. Travelling in time meant violating the laws of nature – which obviously entails risk. But she couldn't believe the timing of Kazu's announcement. A sinkhole had just opened up on the final strait to the finish line. Not that she was going to get cold feet – not after she had come this far. She looked apprehensively into Kazu's eyes.

'What? What will happen?'

'If you don't drink all the coffee before it gets cold . . .'

'. . . If I don't drink the coffee?'

'It will be your turn to be the ghost sitting in this seat.'

A bolt of lightning went off inside Fumiko's head. 'Seriously?'

'The woman who was sitting there just now . . .'

'Broke that rule?'

'Yes. She had gone to meet her dead husband. She must have lost track of the time. When she finally noticed, the coffee had gone cold.'

'. . . and she became a ghost?'

'Yes.'

This is riskier than I imagined, Fumiko thought. There were lots of annoying rules. To have met a ghost and to have been cursed was extraordinary. But now the stakes were even higher.

OK, I can return to the past. Yet, I only have until just before my coffee goes cold. I have no idea how long it takes for a hot coffee to go cold – it's not going to be that long, though. At least it will be long enough to drink my coffee, even if it tastes awful. So, I don't have to worry about that. But say I don't drink it, and I turn into a ghost – that's pretty worrying. Now let's assume I am not going to change the present by going back to the past, no matter how much I try – there's no risk there . . . There are probably no pluses, but there are no minuses either.

Turning into a ghost, on the other hand, is a definite minus.

Fumiko felt herself wavering. She was assailed by countless worries – the most immediate of which was that the coffee that Kazu poured would be revolting. She felt she should be able to handle the taste of coffee. *But what if it is really peppery? What if it is wasabi-flavoured coffee? How could I possibly drink an entire cup of that?*

Realizing her thoughts were becoming paranoid, she shook her head to try to dispel the wave of anxiety that had come over her.

'Fine. I just have to drink the coffee before it goes cold, right?'

'Yes.'

Her mind was made up. Or, more accurately, a stubborn resolve had taken root.

Kazu just stood there impassively. Fumiko could imagine that if she had instead told her, *Sorry, I can't go through with this,* her reaction would have been the same. She briefly closed her eyes, placed her clenched fists on her lap, and drew in a deep breath through her nostrils as if trying to centre herself.

'I'm ready,' she announced. She looked Kazu in the eye. 'Please pour the coffee.'

Giving a small nod, Kazu picked up the silver kettle from the tray with her right hand. She looked at Fumiko demurely. 'Just remember. Drink the coffee before it goes cold,' she whispered.

Kazu began to pour the coffee into the cup. She gave off an air of nonchalance, but her fluid and graceful movements made Fumiko feel like she was observing an ancient ceremony.

Just as Fumiko noticed the shimmering steam rising from the coffee that filled the cup, everything around the table also began to curl up and become indistinguishable from the swirling vapour. She began to feel fear and closed her eyes. The sensation that she was shimmering and becoming distorted, like the rising steam, became even more powerful. She clenched her fists tighter. *If this continues, I won't find myself in the present or past; I'll simply vanish in a wisp of smoke.* As this anxiety engulfed her, she brought to mind the first time she met Goro.

Fumiko first met Goro two years ago, in the spring. She was twenty-six, three years older than him, and stationed at a client company. Goro had been posted to the same place, but worked for another company. Fumiko was the project director and in charge of all visiting employees.

Fumiko never held back if she had something critical to say, even if it was to a superior. She had even gone as far as to get into arguments with senior colleagues. But no one ever spoke critically of her. She was always honest and direct, and her willingness to spare no effort in her work was well admired.

Although Goro was three years her junior, he gave the impression of someone in their thirties. To be blunt, he looked much older than he was. At first Fumiko had felt junior to him and spoke to him in a polite manner accordingly. Furthermore, even though Goro was the youngest in the team, he was the most competent. He was a highly skilled engineer who went about his work silently, and Fumiko saw she could depend on him.

The project Fumiko was leading was almost finished. But just before the delivery date, a serious bug was discovered. There was an error or flaw in the program, and when programming for medical systems, even seemingly trivial bugs are serious. Delivery of the system in this state was impossible. But finding the cause of a bug is like distilling and removing a drop of ink that has fallen in a twenty-five-metre swimming pool. Not only were they facing a daunting and enormous task, they didn't have enough time to do it.

As she was the project director, the responsibility to fulfil the conditions of delivery fell on her shoulders. Delivery was due in one week. As the general consensus was that it would take at least a month to fix the bug, everyone was resigned to missing the deadline. Fumiko thought she would have to tender her resignation. Amid this turmoil, Goro disappeared from the project worksite without telling anyone, and no one could get hold of him. One snide comment led to another and soon everyone suspected that the bug was his fault. People speculated that he must be feeling so ashamed that he couldn't show his face.

Of course, there was nothing concrete to suggest that it had been his mistake. It was simply that if the project was going to be liable for a big loss, it was convenient for it to be someone's fault. As he was the one who was missing, he became the scapegoat, and naturally Fumiko was among those who suspected him. But on the fourth day of no contact, he suddenly appeared with the news that he had found the bug.

He hadn't shaved, and he didn't smell very nice, but no one even considered giving him a hard time for that. Judging by his exhausted face, he probably hadn't even slept. While every other member of the team, including Fumiko, had decided it was too difficult and simply given up, Goro had succeeded in solving the problem. It was nothing less than a miracle. By taking leave without permission and not contacting anyone about it, he had violated basic rules that applied to any company employee. Yet he had demonstrated a commitment to his work that was greater than anyone else's, and he had succeeded as a programmer where no one else could.

After Fumiko expressed her heartfelt gratitude and apologized for thinking even for an instant that it was his mistake, Goro simply smiled as she bowed her head.

'All right then, perhaps you could buy me a coffee?' he said.

That was the moment Fumiko fell in love.

After successfully delivering the system, their new postings were at different companies, and she hardly saw him. But she believed in getting things done. Whenever she could spare the time, she would take him to different places, each time on the pretext of buying him a coffee.

Goro's approach to work was obsessive. When he started working towards a goal, he wouldn't see anything else. Fumiko first learned that TIP-G had its headquarters in America when she visited his home. He talked so enthusiastically about working for TIP-G, and it made her worry. *When his dream comes true, which will he choose: his dream or me? I mustn't think like that, there's no comparison. But gosh . . .*

Then, little by little, it became clearer to her how big a loss it would be. She could no longer bring herself to try to ascertain how he felt about her. Time passed, and that spring, he finally got an offer to work at TIP-G. His dream had come true.

Fumiko's anxiety was justified. Goro had chosen to go to America. He had chosen his dream. She had learned this a week ago, at this cafe. Now she opened her eyes feeling disorientated, as if waking from a dream.

The sensation that she was a spirit, shimmering and swirling like steam, now left her, and she began to regain awareness of her limbs. In a panic, she felt her body and face, to make sure it was herself who had appeared. When she came to her senses, a man was there before her, watching her strange behaviour, puzzled.

It was Goro, unless she was mistaken. Goro, who was meant to be in America, was there before her eyes. She really had returned to the past. She understood the puzzlement on his face. There was no doubt that she had returned to a week ago. The inside of the cafe was just how she remembered it.

The man called Fusagi had a magazine spread out on the table closest to the door. Hirai was sitting at the counter, and Kazu was there. And opposite her was Goro, at the same table where they had been. But just one thing was wrong – the seat in which Fumiko sat.

A week ago, she had been sitting facing Goro. Now, however, she was in the seat of the woman in the dress. She was still facing Goro, but they were now one table apart. *He's so far away.* His puzzled look was completely justified.

But unnatural or not, she couldn't leave her seat. That was one of the rules. *But what if he asks why I am sitting here? What should I say?* Fumiko gulped at the thought.

'Oh gosh, is that the time? Sorry, I have to go.'

Goro may have looked perplexed, but despite their now unnatural seating positions, he had said the exact words she had heard a week ago. This must be an unspoken rule when travelling back to the past.

'Ah, that's OK. That's OK. You don't have any more time, do you? I don't have much time either.'

'What?'

'Sorry.'

They weren't on the same page and the conversation wasn't going anywhere. Although she knew the moment she had returned to, Fumiko was still confused – it was, after all, the first time she had returned to the past.

To give herself time to settle, she took a sip of the coffee while looking up from under her brows to observe Goro's expression.

Oh no! The coffee is already lukewarm! It will be cold in no time!

Fumiko was dismayed. At this temperature, she could already have gulped it down. This was an unexpected setback. She scowled at Kazu. She hated the way Kazu permanently wore such a deadpan expression. But that was not all . . .

'Ugh . . . So bitter.'

The taste was even bitterer than she had anticipated. It was the bitterest coffee she had ever drunk. Goro looked confused at hearing Fumiko's strange utterance.

Rubbing above his right eyebrow, Goro looked at his watch. He was worried about the time. Fumiko understood that. She was in a hurry too.

'Um . . . I have something important to say,' she said hurriedly.

Fumiko shovelled sugar into her cup from the sugar pot placed in front of her. Then, after adding a fair amount of milk, she clinked and clanged her cup with her spoon with her vigorous stirring.

'What?' Goro frowned.

Fumiko wasn't sure if the frown was because she was adding too much sugar, or because he didn't want to talk about anything important just then.

'What I mean is . . . I want to talk about this properly.'

Goro looked at his watch.

'Hang on a sec . . .' Fumiko took a sip of the coffee that she had sweetened. She nodded in approval. She hadn't drunk coffee until she met Goro. It had been the pretext of buying him a coffee that led to their dates. The curious sight of Fumiko, who hated coffee, frantically adding a tremendous amount of sugar and milk earned her a wry smile from Goro.

'Hey, this is a serious situation, and you're just smirking at me drinking coffee.'

'No I'm not.'

'You blatantly are! You can't deny it, I can tell by looking at your face.'

Fumiko regretted interrupting the flow of the conversation. She had gone to the effort of returning to the past, and now it was going the same way as a week earlier. She was again chasing him away with her childish talk.

Goro got up from his seat, looking agitated. He called to Kazu behind the counter.

'Excuse me . . . How much, please?' He reached for the bill.

Fumiko knew that if she didn't do something, Goro would pay and then leave. 'Wait!'

'It's fine, let's leave it at that.'

'This isn't what I came to say.'

'What?'

(*Don't go.*)

'Why didn't you talk about it with me?'

(*I don't want you to go.*)

'Well, that's . . .'

'I know how much your work means to you. I don't necessarily mind if you go to America. I won't stand in the way.'

(*I thought we were going to be together for ever.*)

'But, at least . . .'

(*Was it only me thinking that?*)

'I wanted you to discuss it with me. You know, it's pretty despicable just deciding without talking about it . . .'

(*I really, truly* . . .)

'That's just . . . well, you know.'

(. . . *loved you.*)

'It makes me feel forgotten . . .'

' . . '

'What I wanted to say was . . .'

' . . '

(*Not that it's going to change anything* . . .)

'Well . . . I just wanted to say that.'

Fumiko had planned to speak honestly – after all, it wouldn't change the present. But she couldn't say it. She felt that saying it would be to admit defeat. She would have hated herself for saying anything like, *Which do you choose – work or me?* Until she had met Goro, she had always put work first. It was the last thing that she wanted to say. She also didn't want to be talking like a parody of a woman, especially to a boyfriend three years her junior – she had her pride. She also was perhaps jealous that his career had overtaken her own. So she hadn't spoken honestly. Anyhow . . . it was too late.

'Fine then, go . . . Whatever . . . It's not as if anything I say will stop you going to America.'

After saying this, Fumiko gulped down the rest of her coffee. 'Whoa.'

When the cup was empty, the dizziness started again. She was once more swallowed up by a wavering and shimmering world.

She began pondering. (*What did I come back for, exactly?*)

'I never thought that I was the right man for you.'

She didn't know why Goro would be saying this.

'When you invited me for coffee,' he continued, 'I always said to myself that I mustn't fall for you . . .'

'What?'

'Because I have this . . .' He ran his fingers through his fringe, which had been combed down to cover the right side of his forehead. He revealed the large burn scar that spread from his right eyebrow to his right ear. 'Before I met you, I always thought women found me repulsive, and I couldn't even talk to them.'

'I . . .'

'Even after we had started dating.'

'*It never even bothered me!*' shouted Fumiko, but she had become one with the vapour and her words didn't reach him.

'I thought that it was only a matter of time before you started liking other, better-looking guys.'

(*Never . . . How can you think that!*)

'I always thought that . . .'

(*Never!*)

It was a shock for Fumiko to hear him confess this for the first time. But now that he mentioned it, it seemed to make sense. The more she loved him, and the more she thought about marriage, the more she could sense some kind of invisible barrier.

When she asked if he loved her, he would nod, but he never said the words *I love you*. When they walked down the street together, Goro would look down sometimes, almost apologetically, and stroke his right eyebrow. Goro had also noticed that men walking down the street were always gawking at her.

(*Surely he hadn't been hung up on that.*)

Yet, as she thought that, Fumiko regretted her own thoughts. While she saw it as his little hang-up, for him it was a painful, long-standing complex.

(*I had no idea he felt that way.*)

Fumiko's awareness was fading. Her body was engulfed in a wavering, dizzy sensation. Goro had picked up the bill and was making his way to the cash register with his bag in his hand.

(*Nothing about the present is going to change. It's right that it is not going to change. He made the right choice. Achieving his dream is worth much more to him than I am. I guess I have to give up on Goro. I'll let him go and wish him success with all my heart.*)

Fumiko was slowly closing her bloodshot eyes when—

'Three years,' Goro said with his back to her. 'Please wait three years. Then I'll return, I promise.'

It was a faint voice, but the cafe was small. Although now only vapour, Fumiko could clearly hear Goro's voice.

'When I return . . .' Goro touched his right eyebrow out of habit and, with his back to Fumiko, said something else that was too muffled to hear.

'Huh? What?'

At that moment, Fumiko's awareness of that place became shimmering steam. Just as she was slipping away, Fumiko saw Goro's face as he glanced back before leaving the cafe. She saw his face for only a split second but he was smiling wonderfully, just like the time when he had said, 'Perhaps you could buy me a coffee?'

When she came to, Fumiko was sitting in the seat, alone in the cafe. She felt as if she had just had a dream, but the coffee cup in front of her was empty. Her mouth still had a sweet taste in it.

Just then, the woman in the dress returned from the toilet. When she caught Fumiko sitting in her chair, she swooped silently up to her.

'Move,' she said in an eerily powerful low voice.

Fumiko started. 'I . . . I'm sorry,' she said, standing up from the chair.

The dreamlike sensation had still not dissipated. Had she really returned to the past?

Going back in time didn't change the present, so it was only normal that nothing felt different. The aroma of coffee drifted from the kitchen. Fumiko turned to look. Kazu had appeared carrying a fresh cup of coffee placed on the tray.

Kazu walked past her as if nothing had happened. When she got to the woman in the dress's table, she cleared Fumiko's used cup and placed the fresh cup of coffee in front of the woman in the dress. The woman gave a small nod of acknowledgement and began to read her book.

Returning to the counter, Kazu asked casually, 'How was it?'

On hearing these words, Fumiko finally felt sure that she had travelled in time. She had returned to that day – one week ago. But if she had . . .

'So I'm just thinking . . .'

'Yes?'

'It doesn't change the present, right?'

'That's right.'

'But what about the things that happen later?'

'I'm not sure what you're saying.'

'From now on . . .' Fumiko chose her words. 'From now on – what about the future?'

Kazu looked straight at Fumiko. 'Well, as the future hasn't

happened yet, I guess that's up to you . . .' she said, revealing a smile for the first time.

Fumiko's eyes lit up.

Kazu stood in front of the cash register. 'Coffee service, plus late-night surcharge, that's four hundred and twenty yen, please,' she said quietly.

Fumiko gave a big nod and went towards the cash register. She felt light-footed. After paying 420 yen, Fumiko looked Kazu in the eye.

'Thank you,' she said and bowed her head low.

Then, after looking around the entire cafe, she once again bowed, not to anyone in particular, more to the cafe itself. Then she walked out of the cafe without a care.

CLANG-DONG

Kazu started entering the money into the cash register, with her deadpan expression, as if nothing out of the ordinary had happened. The woman in the dress gave a slight smile as she quietly closed the book, a novel titled *The Lovers*.

II

Husband and Wife

The cafe has no air conditioning. It opened in 1874, more than a hundred and forty years ago. Back then, people still used oil lamps for light. Over the years, the cafe underwent a few small renovations, but its interior today is pretty much unchanged from its original look. When it opened, the decor must have been considered very avant-garde. The commonly accepted date for the appearance of the modern cafe in Japan is around 1888 – a whole fourteen years later.

Coffee was introduced to Japan in the Edo period, around the late seventeenth century. Initially it didn't appeal to Japanese taste buds and it was certainly not thought of as something one drank for enjoyment – which was no wonder, considering it tasted like black, bitter water.

When electricity was introduced, the cafe switched the oil lamps for electric lights, but installing an air conditioner would have destroyed the charm of the interior. So, to this day, the cafe has no air conditioning.

But every year, summer comes around. When midday temperatures soar to above 30 degrees Celsius, you would expect a shop, even one that is underground, to be sweltering inside. The cafe does have a large-bladed ceiling fan, which, being electric, must have been added later. But a ceiling fan like this one doesn't generate a strong breeze and simply serves to make the air circulate.

The hottest temperature ever recorded in Japan was 41 degrees Celsius at Ekawasaki in Kochi Prefecture. It is difficult to imagine a ceiling fan being at all useful in such heat. But even in the height of summer, this cafe is always pleasantly cool. Who is keeping it cool? Beyond the staff, no one knows – nor will they ever know.

It was an afternoon in summer. It was only early in the season but the temperature outside was as high as on any midsummer day. Inside the cafe, a young woman seated at the counter was busy writing. Next to her was an iced coffee diluted by melting ice. The woman was dressed for summer, in a white frilled T-shirt, a tight grey miniskirt, and strappy sandals. She sat with her back straight, as her pen raced across cherry-blossom-pink letter paper.

Standing behind the counter, a slender woman of pale complexion looked on, her eyes filled with a youthful sparkle. It was Kei Tokita, and the contents of the letter had no doubt piqued her curiosity. Occasionally she would take sneak peeks with a look of childlike fascination on her face.

Apart from the woman at the counter who was writing the letter, the other customers in the cafe were the woman in the white dress sitting in *that* chair, and the man named Fusagi, who was sitting at the table seat closest to the entrance. Fusagi once again had a magazine opened on the table.

The woman writing the letter drew a deep breath. Kei followed by taking a deep breath herself.

'Sorry for being here so long,' the woman said, inserting her finished letter in an envelope.

'Not at all,' Kei said, fleetingly glancing down at her feet.

'Um . . . Do you think you could pass this to my sister?'

The woman was grasping the letter-filled envelope with two hands, and presenting it to Kei politely. Her name was Kumi Hirai. She was the younger sister of the cafe regular Yaeko Hirai.

'Ah. Well, if I know your sister . . .' Kei thought the better of continuing, and bit her lip.

Kumi tilted her head slightly and gave Kei an inquisitive look.

But Kei simply smiled as if she meant nothing by it. 'OK . . . I'll pass it on to her,' she said, looking at the letter Kumi was holding.

Kumi hesitated a little. 'I know she might not even read it. But if you could . . .' she said, bowing her head low.

Kei assumed a correct and polite stance. 'Of course I will,' she said, acting as if she was being entrusted with something extremely important. She received the letter with both hands and made a courteous bow while Kumi moved to the cash register.

'How much?' Kumi asked, handing Kei the bill.

Kei carefully placed the letter on the counter. Then she took the bill and began punching the keys of the cash register.

This cafe's cash register had to be a contender for the oldest one still in use – although it hadn't been in the cafe right from the beginning. Its keys were much like those of a typewriter, and it was introduced to the cafe at the beginning of the Showa period, in about 1925. This was a very solidly built cash register, designed to prevent theft. Its frame alone weighed about forty kilograms. It made a noisy *clank* each time a key was punched.

'Coffee and . . . toast . . . curry rice . . . mixed parfait . . .'

Clank clank clank clank . . . clank clank. Kei rhythmically punched in the amounts of each order. 'Ice-cream soda . . . pizza toast . . .'

Kumi certainly seemed to have eaten a lot. In fact, not everything fitted on one bill. Kei began punching in the orders of the second bill. 'Curry pilaf . . . banana float . . . cutlet curry . . .' Normally it's not necessary to read out each item, but Kei didn't mind doing it. The sight of her punching in the amounts resembled a child happily immersed in playing with a toy.

'Then you had the Gorgonzola gnocchi, and the chicken and perilla cream pasta . . .'

'I sort of pigged out, didn't I?' said Kumi in a rather loud voice, perhaps a little embarrassed at having everything read out. *Please, you don't have to read it all out*, was probably what she wanted to say.

'You certainly did.'

Of course, it wasn't Kei who said this – it was Fusagi. Having heard the order being read out, he had muttered this softly while he continued to read his magazine.

Kei ignored him, but Kumi's ears went a rosy pink. 'How much?' Kumi asked. But Kei had not finished.

'Ah, let's see . . . then there was the mixed sandwich . . .

grilled onigiri . . . second curry rice . . . and er . . . the iced coffee . . . comes to a total . . . of ten thousand, two hundred and thirty yen.'

Kei smiled, her round sparkling eyes showing nothing but kindness.

'OK then, here you go,' Kumi said, and she quickly pulled out two notes from her purse.

Kei took the notes and counted them efficiently. 'Receiving eleven thousand yen,' she said, and again she punched the keys of the cash register.

Kumi waited with her head hung low.

Cha-ching . . . The cash drawer opened with a jolt and Kei pulled out the change.

'That's seven hundred and seventy yen change.'

Smiling once again, with her round eyes sparkling, Kei gave Kumi the change.

Kumi bowed her head politely. 'Thank you. It was delicious.'

Perhaps because she was embarrassed that all the things she had eaten had been read aloud, Kumi now seemed eager to leave quickly. But just as she was going, Kei called out to stop her.

'Um . . . Kumi,' she said.

Kumi stopped in her tracks and looked back at her.

'About your sister . . .' Kei said, and glanced down at her feet. 'Is there any message you would like me to give her?' She held both hands up in the air as she asked.

'No it's OK. I wrote it in the letter,' Kumi said, without hesitation.

'Yes, I imagine you did.' Kei furrowed her brow as if disappointed.

Perhaps touched that Kei showed such concern, Kumi grinned and said, after a moment's thought, 'Perhaps there is one thing you could say . . .'

'Yes of course.' Kei's expression brightened instantly.

'Tell her that neither Dad nor Mum is angry any more.'

'Your father and mother aren't angry any more,' Kei repeated.

'Yes . . . Please tell her that.'

Kei's eyes were once again round and sparkling. She nodded twice. 'OK, I will,' she said happily.

Kumi looked around the cafe and once more bowed politely to Kei before she left.

CLANG-DONG

Kei went over to the entrance to check that Kumi had gone, and then with a quick pirouette, she started talking to the vacant counter.

'Did you have a fight with your parents?'

Then from under the supposedly vacant counter a husky voice answered. 'They disowned me,' Hirai said, emerging from under the counter.

'But you heard her, right?'

'Heard what?'

'That your father and mother aren't cross any more.'

'I'll believe that when I see it . . .'

After being crouched under the counter for a really long time, Hirai was bent over like an old woman. She hobbled out into the room. As always, she had her curlers in. She was dolled up in a leopard-print camisole, a tight pink skirt, and beach sandals.

Hirai winced a little. 'Your sister seems really nice.'

'When you're not in my position, I'm sure she is . . . yeah.'

Hirai sat on the counter seat where Kumi had been sitting. She plucked a cigarette from her leopard-print pouch and lit it. A plume of smoke rose into the air. Following it with her eyes, Hirai's face showed a rare vulnerability. She looked as if her thoughts had drifted somewhere far away.

Kei walked around Hirai to take her position behind the counter. 'Do you want to talk about it?' she asked.

Hirai blew another plume of smoke. 'She resents me.'

'What do you mean she resents you?' Kei asked.

'She didn't want it passed down to her.'

'Huh?' Kei tilted her head sideways, unsure what Hirai was talking about.

'The inn . . .'

The inn Hirai's family ran was a well-known luxury place in Sendai, Miyagi Prefecture. Her parents had planned for Hirai to take over the inn, but she had a falling out with them thirteen years earlier and it was decided that Kumi would be the successor. Her parents were in good health, but they were getting on in years and as the future manager, Kumi had already taken over many of the inn's responsibilities. Since Kumi had accepted she would take over, she regularly made the trek to Tokyo to visit Hirai and try and persuade her to come home.

'I keep telling her I don't want to go home. But she keeps on asking time and time and time again.' Hirai bent the fingers of both hands one by one as if she was counting the times. 'Saying that she was persistent would be an understatement.'

'But you don't have to hide from her.'

'I don't want to see it.'

'See what?'

'Her face.'

Kei tilted her head inquisitively.

'I see it written on her face. Because of what I did, she is now going to be the owner of an inn she doesn't want to run. She wants me to come home so that she can be free,' Hirai said.

'I don't really see how all that can be written on her face,' Kei suggested doubtfully.

Hirai knew Kei well enough to know she was probably struggling to picture this. Her very literal mind sometimes missed the point.

'What I mean,' Hirai said, 'is it just feels like she is pressuring me.'

Frowning, she blew out another plume of smoke.

Kei stood there thoughtfully tilting her head to the side several times.

'Oh god! Is that the time? Oh dear!' Hirai said dramatically. She quickly stubbed out her cigarette in the ashtray. 'I've got a bar to open.' She stood up and gingerly stretched from the hips. 'You sure feel it in your back after three hours crouched down like that.'

Hirai thumped her lower back and headed quickly for the entrance, her beach sandals flip-flopping loudly.

'Hold on! The letter.' Kei picked up the letter Kumi had given her and presented it to Hirai.

'Throw it away!' Hirai said, without looking, waving it away dismissively with her right hand.

'You're not going to read it?'

'I can imagine what it says. *It's really tough for me by myself.*

Please come home. It's OK if you learn the ropes once you're there.
You know, that sort of stuff.'

As she spoke, Hirai pulled out her dictionary-sized purse
from her leopard-print pouch. She put the money for the
coffee on the counter.

'See you later,' she said and left the cafe, clearly desperate
to get away.

CLANG-DONG

'I can't just throw it away.' Kei's face showed her dilemma as
she looked at the letter from Kumi.

CLANG-DONG

While Kei was still standing frozen like this, the bell rang again
and Kazu Tokita entered the cafe, taking the place of Hirai.

Kazu had gone out today with Nagare, the cafe's owner and her
cousin, to buy supplies. She returned carrying several shopping bags in both hands. The car key was jangling with other
keys on the key ring hanging off her ring finger. She was dressed
casually, wearing a T-shirt and blue jeans. This was in stark
contrast to the bow tie and apron she wore when working.

'Welcome back,' smiled Kei, still holding the letter.

'Sorry we took so long.'

'No, it was fine. It was pretty quiet.'

'I'll get changed right away.' Kazu's face was always more
expressive before she put on her bow tie. She stuck out her
tongue cheekily and darted into the back room.

Kei kept holding the letter. 'Where's that damn husband of mine?' she called out to the back room, looking at the entrance.

Kazu and Nagare did the shopping together. This wasn't because there was so much to buy, but because Nagare was a difficult shopper. He would get so caught up with wanting to buy the best that he would often go over budget. It was Kazu's job to tag along and make sure he didn't. While they were gone, Kei handled the cafe alone. Sometimes when Nagare was unable to find the ingredients he wanted, he would get in a stink and go out drinking.

'He said he would probably be late coming back,' Kazu said.

'Oh, I bet he's gone out drinking again.'

Kazu poked her head out. 'I'll take over now,' she said apologetically.

'Argh . . . I don't believe that man!' Kei said, puffing out her cheeks. She retreated to the back room, still holding the letter.

The only people left in the cafe were the woman in the dress quietly reading her novel and Fusagi. Despite it being summer, they were both drinking hot coffee. There were two reasons for this: firstly, you received free refills with hot coffee, and secondly the coffee being hot didn't bother these two customers as it was always cool inside the cafe, and they sat there for so long anyway. Kazu soon reappeared dressed in her normal waitress's uniform.

Summer had only just begun, but today it was over 30 degrees Celsius outside. She had walked less than a hundred metres from the car park but the sweat still beaded on her face. She exhaled sharply while wiping her brow with a handkerchief.

'Um, excuse me . . .' said Fusagi, who had lifted his head from his magazine.

'Yes?' said Kazu, as if something had surprised her.

'May I have a refill, please?'

'Oh, sure.' She let her usual cool demeanour slip, and replied in the casual tone she had used while wearing a T-shirt just earlier.

Fusagi had his eyes glued on Kazu as she walked into the kitchen. When he came to the cafe, Fusagi always sat in the same chair. If another customer was sitting there, he would leave rather than sit anywhere else. Rather than coming every day, he normally made an appearance two or three times a week, some time after lunch. He would open up his travel magazine and look through it from cover to cover while occasionally jotting down notes. He would usually stay as long as it took to finish the magazine. The only thing he ever ordered was a hot coffee.

The coffee served at the cafe was made from mocha beans grown in Ethiopia, which have a distinct aroma. But it didn't appeal to everybody's tastes – though it was deliciously aromatic, some found its bitter fruitiness and complex overtones a little overbearing. On Nagare's insistence, the cafe only served mocha. Fusagi happened to like this coffee, and he seemed to find the cafe a comfortable space to leisurely read his magazine. Kazu returned from the kitchen holding the glass carafe to pour Fusagi his refill.

Standing by his table, Kazu picked up the cup by the saucer. Fusagi would normally continue to read his magazine while waiting for her to pour his refill – but today was different: he looked directly at her with a strange expression.

Sensing that his manner was different from usual, she thought he must want something else besides the coffee refill. 'Is there anything else?' she asked with a smile.

He smiled at her politely, looking a little embarrassed. 'Are you a new waitress here?' he asked.

Her expression didn't change as she placed the cup in front of Fusagi. 'Er . . . hmm,' was all that she replied.

'Oh, really?' he replied a little bashfully. He seemed pleased to have communicated to the waitress that he was a regular customer. But satisfied with that, he immediately lowered his head and returned to reading his magazine.

Kazu went about her work with a deadpan expression as if nothing was out of the ordinary. But with no other customers, there was not much to do. Her only work at that moment was wiping some washed glasses and plates with a tea towel and returning them to the shelf. As she went about this task, she started talking to Fusagi. In this small, intimate cafe, it was quite easy to hold a conversation from such a distance without raising one's voice.

'So, do you come here often?'

He lifted his head. 'Yes.'

She went on. 'Do you know about this place? Have you heard its urban legend?'

'Yes, I know all about it.'

'About *that* seat as well?'

'Yes.'

'So are you one of those customers planning on going back in time?'

'Yes, I am,' he replied without hesitation.

She let her hands pause briefly. 'If you return to the past, what are you planning to do?' But realizing the question was too intrusive and not something she would normally ask, she immediately backtracked. 'That was a rude thing to ask. I'm sorry . . .' She bowed her head and returned to her wiping, avoiding his gaze.

He looked at her with her head bowed, and quietly picked up his zipped portfolio. From it, he pulled out a plain brown envelope. Its four corners were crumpled as though he had been carrying it around for a long time. There was no address on the envelope, but it looked like a letter.

He held this letter tentatively in both hands, holding it up a little in front of his chest for her to see.

'What's that?' she asked, pausing once again in what she was doing.

'For my wife,' he muttered in a quiet voice. 'It's for my wife.'

'Is that a letter?'

'Yeah.'

'For your wife?'

'Yeah, I never managed to give it to her.'

'So, you want to return to the day you meant to pass it to her?'

'Yeah, that's right,' he answered, once again without any hesitation.

'So, where is your wife now?' she asked.

Rather than answering straight away, he paused in awkward silence. 'Um . . .'

She stood looking squarely at him, waiting for him to answer.

'I don't know,' he said in a barely discernible voice as he

began to scratch his head. After this admission his expression hardened.

She said nothing in reply.

Then, as if offering an excuse, he said, 'Hmm, but, I really had a wife,' and then he hastily added, 'Her name was . . .' He began tapping his head with his finger. 'Huh? That's odd.' He tilted his head. 'What was her name?' he said, and went quiet again.

At some time during this, Kei had returned from the back room. Her face looked drained, maybe because she had just witnessed Kazu and Fusagi's exchange.

'Well that's odd. I'm sorry,' Fusagi said, forcing an awkward smile.

Kazu's face showed a subtle mix of emotions – it wasn't quite her normal cool expression, but nor was she showing much empathy.

'Don't worry about it . . .' she said.

CLANG-DONG

Kazu silently looked to the entrance.

'Ah,' she gasped when she saw Kohtake standing in the doorway.

Kohtake worked as a nurse at the local hospital. She must have been on her way home. Instead of her nurse's uniform, she was wearing an olive-green tunic and navy-blue capri pants. She had a black shoulder bag on one shoulder, and she was wiping the sweat from her brow with a lilac handkerchief. Kohtake casually acknowledged Kei and Kazu standing behind the counter before walking up to Fusagi's table.

'Hello, Fusagi, I see you're here again today,' she said.

Hearing his name, he looked up at Kohtake in puzzlement, before averting his eyes and lowering his head in silence.

Kohtake sensed that his mood was different from usual. She supposed he might not be feeling very well. 'Fusagi, are you OK?' she asked gently.

Fusagi lifted his head and looked directly at her. 'I'm sorry. Have we met before?' he asked apologetically.

Kohtake lost her smile. In a cold silence, the lilac handkerchief she had just used to wipe her brow dropped from her hand onto the floor.

Fusagi had early onset Alzheimer's disease, and was losing his memory. The disease causes rapid depletion of the brain's neural cells. The brain pathologically atrophies, causing loss of intelligence and changes to the personality. One of the striking symptoms of early onset Alzheimer's is how the deterioration of brain function appears so sporadic. Sufferers forget some things but remember other things. In Fusagi's case, his memories were gradually disappearing, starting with the most recent. Meanwhile, his previously hard-to-please personality had been slowing mellowing.

In that moment, Fusagi remembered that he had a wife, but he didn't remember that Kohtake, standing before him, *was* his wife.

'I guess not,' Kohtake said quietly as she took one, then two steps back.

Kazu stared at Kohtake, while Kei pointed her pale face down at the floor. Kohtake slowly turned round and walked to the seat at the counter that was furthest from Fusagi and sat down.

It was after sitting down that she noticed the handkerchief that had dropped from her hand. She decided to ignore it and pretend it wasn't hers. But Fusagi noticed the handkerchief, which had fallen near his feet, and picked it up. He stared at it in his hand for a while, and then he rose from his chair and walked over to the counter where Kohtake was sitting.

'You'll have to excuse me. Recently I've been forgetting a lot,' he said bowing his head.

Kohtake didn't look at him. 'OK,' she said. She took the handkerchief in her trembling hand.

Fusagi bowed his head again and shuffled awkwardly back to his seat. He sat down but couldn't relax. After turning several pages of his magazine, he paused and scratched his head. Then a few moments later, he reached for his coffee and took one sip. The cup had only just been refilled, but—

'Damn coffee's cold,' he muttered.

'Another refill?' Kazu asked.

But he stood up in a hurry. 'I'll be leaving now,' he said abruptly, closing his magazine and putting away his things.

Kohtake continued to stare at the floor with her hands on her lap as she clenched the handkerchief tightly.

Fusagi moved to the cash register and handed over the bill. 'How much?'

'Three hundred and eighty yen, please,' Kazu said, glancing sideways at Kohtake. She punched in the amount on the cash-register keys.

'Three hundred and eighty yen.' Fusagi pulled out a thousand-yen note from his well-worn leather wallet. 'Right, here's a thousand,' he said as he handed the note over.

'Receiving one thousand yen,' Kazu said, taking the money and punching the cash-register keys.

Fusagi kept glancing at Kohtake, but with no apparent purpose. He appeared to be just restlessly looking around while waiting for the change.

'That's six hundred and twenty yen change.'

Fusagi quickly reached out his hand and took the change. 'Thanks for the coffee,' he said, almost apologetically, and hurried out.

CLANG-DONG

'Thank you, come again . . .'

Upon Fusagi's departure, the cafe fell into an uncomfortable silence. The woman in the dress quietly read her book, unbothered as ever with what was going on around her. With no background music playing, the only sounds that could be heard were the constant ticking of the clocks and the woman in the dress occasionally turning the page of her book.

Kazu first broke this long silence. 'Kohtake . . .' she said. But she was unable to find the appropriate words.

'It's OK, I have been mentally preparing for today.' Kohtake smiled at Kei and Kazu. 'Don't worry.'

But after speaking she once again looked down at the floor.

She had explained Fusagi's illness to Kei and Kazu before, and Nagare and Hirai knew about it too. She had resigned herself to the fact that one day he would completely forget who she was. She was always preparing herself. If it happens, she thought, I will care for him as a nurse. I am a nurse, so I can do that.

Early onset Alzheimer's disease progresses differently for each individual, depending on a whole range of factors which include age, gender, the cause of the illness, and the treatment. Fusagi's rate of deterioration was progressing rapidly.

Kohtake was still in shock from his forgetting who she was. She was struggling to get things straight in her head while the general mood was so low. She turned to Kei, but she was in the kitchen. Almost instantly, she appeared holding a half-gallon bottle of sake.

'A gift from a customer,' Kei said as she put it down on the table. 'Drink, anyone?' she asked, with smiling eyes, still red from crying. The name on the label was *Seven Happinesses*.

Kei's spur-of-the-moment decision had introduced a ray of light into the gloomy atmosphere, and eased the tension between the three.

Kohtake was in two minds about drinking, but was reluctant to pass up the chance. 'Well, just one . . .' she said.

Kohtake was simply thankful that the mood had changed. She had heard that Kei often acted on impulse, but she had never expected to experience her sense of fun at a moment like this.

Hirai had often mentioned *Kei's talent for living happily*; she may have looked despondent a few moments earlier, but now she was looking at Kohtake with wide, bright eyes. Kohtake found staring into those eyes a strangely calming experience.

'I'll see if I can find some nibbles to go with it,' Kazu said, disappearing into the kitchen.

'Why don't we warm the sake?'

'No, it's OK.'

'Right, we'll drink it as it is.'

Kei removed the lid deftly and poured the sake into the row of glasses she had set out.

Kohtake let out a chuckle as Kei placed a glass in front of her. 'Thank you,' she said with a thin smile.

Kazu returned with a tin of pickles. 'This was all I could find . . .' She put down a small dish, tipped the pickles onto it and set three small forks on the counter.

'Oh, yum!' Kei said. 'But I can't drink myself.' She brought out a carton of orange juice from the fridge under the counter and poured herself a glass.

None of the three women were that particular about sake, especially Kei, who didn't drink. Seven Happinesses earned its name from the claim that those who drank it would obtain seven different kinds of happiness. It was transparent, pigment-free top-shelf sake. The two drinkers did not take much notice of this premium sake's subtle glacial hue – nor its fruity aroma. But it went down well and delivered on the happy feeling its label promised.

As Kohtake inhaled the sweet aroma, she recalled one summer day, some fifteen years ago, when she first visited the cafe.

There had been a heat wave in Japan that summer. Record temperatures were continually reported throughout the country. Day after day, the television discussed the unusual weather, often alluding to global warming. Fusagi had taken a day off from work, and they had gone shopping together. That day was a real scorcher. Hot and bothered from the heat, Fusagi pleaded that they take refuge somewhere cool, and together they searched for a suitable place, like a cafe. The problem was that everyone had the same idea. None of the cafes or family restaurants they spotted had empty seats.

By chance, they saw a small sign in a narrow back alley. The cafe's name was Funiculi Funicula. It was the same name as a song Kohtake once knew. It was a long time since she'd heard it, but she still remembered the melody clearly. The lyrics were about climbing a volcano. The thought of red-hot lava on this hot summer day made everything seem even hotter and jewel-like beads of sweat formed on Kohtake's brow. However, when they opened the heavy wooden door and entered, the cafe was refreshingly cool. The *clang-dong* of the bell was also comfort-ing. And, even though it had three two-seater tables and a three-seater counter, the only customer there was a woman in a white dress seated furthest from the entrance. Thanks to a stroke of luck, they had made a real find.

'What a relief,' Fusagi said and chose the table closest to the entrance. He quickly ordered iced coffee from the woman with the bright eyes who brought them glasses of cold water. 'Iced coffee for me too, please,' Kohtake said, sitting opposite him. Fusagi must have been uncomfortable with this seating arrangement, as he moved and sat at the counter. This didn't upset Kohtake: she was used to such behaviour from him. She was just thinking how wonderful it was to find such a relaxing cafe so close to the hospital where she worked.

The thick pillars and the massive wooden beam that cut across the ceiling were a lustrous dark brown, like the colour of chestnuts. Mounted on the walls were three large wall clocks. Kohtake didn't know much about antiques but she could tell that these were from an earlier period. The walls were tan, made of earthen plaster with a wonderful patina of obscure stains that had obviously built up over many years. It was daytime outside, but in this windowless cafe, there was no sense of time. Dim lighting gave the cafe a sepia hue. All this created a comforting, retro atmosphere.

It had been incredibly cool in the cafe, but there was no sign of an air conditioner. A wooden-bladed fan fixed to the ceiling was slowly rotating, but that was all. Thinking how strange it was that this cafe was so cool, Kohtake asked both Kei and Nagare about it. Neither provided satisfactory answers; they just said, 'It's been like this since long ago.'

Kohtake took a real shine to the atmosphere, and to the personalities of Kei and the others. And so she began to come often during her breaks from work.

'Chee—' Kazu was going to say *Cheers* but stopped herself, screwing up her face as if she had committed a faux pas.

'I guess it's not a celebration, is it?'

'Oh, come on. Let's not be too down,' Kei said glumly. She turned to Kohtake and smiled sympathetically.

Kohtake held up her glass in front of Kazu's. 'I'm sorry.'

'No, it's fine.'

Kohtake smiled reassuringly and clinked glasses with her. This harmonious clink – unexpected and cheerful – sounded throughout the room. Kohtake took a sip of Seven Happinesses. Its gentle sweetness spread through her mouth. 'It's been half a year since he started calling me by my maiden name . . .' she began, speaking softly. 'It's silently progressing. Fading away, slowly but steadily fading away . . . His memory of me, that is.' She laughed softly. 'I have been mentally preparing for this, you know,' she said.

As Kei listened, her eyes were again slowly reddening.

'But it's really OK . . . honestly,' Kohtake hastened to add, waving her hand reassuringly. 'Hey guys, I'm a nurse. Look, even if my identity is totally erased from his memory, I'll be part of his life as a nurse. I'll still be there for him.'

Kohtake had put on her most confident voice to reassure Kei and Kazu. She meant what she said. She was putting on a brave face, but her bravery was real. *I can still be there for him because I'm a nurse.*

Kazu was playing with her glass, staring at it with a deadpan expression.

Kei's eyes welled up again and a single teardrop fell.

Flap.

The sound came from behind Kohtake. The woman in the dress had closed her book.

Kohtake turned round to see the woman in the dress placing the closed novel on the table. She took a handkerchief from her white purse, rose from the table and headed towards the toilet. The woman in the dress walked silently. Had they not heard the novel close, they might never even have noticed she had gone.

Kohtake's eyes stayed glued to her movements, but Kei just glanced at her, and Kazu took a sip of Seven Happinesses and didn't even look up. After all, it was just an ordinary daily occurrence for them.

'That reminds me. I wonder why Fusagi wants to return to the past?' Kohtake said, staring at the seat vacated by the woman in the dress. She knew, of course, that *that* was the seat for returning to the past.

Before the Alzheimer's disease took hold, Fusagi was not the type of person who believed in such tales. When Kohtake casually mentioned the rumour that this cafe could send you back to the past, he would scoff. He didn't believe in ghosts or the paranormal.

But after he started to lose his memory, the once-sceptical Fusagi started coming to the cafe and waiting for the woman in the dress to leave her seat. When Kohtake first heard of this, she found it hard to believe. But personality change is one of the symptoms of Alzheimer's, and now that the disease had progressed, Fusagi had newly become very absent-minded. In light of such changes, Kohtake had decided that it wasn't particularly strange that he had changed what he believed in.

But why did he want to return to the past?

Kohtake was very curious about this. She had asked him on several occasions, but he just said, 'It's a secret.'

'Apparently he wants to give you a letter,' Kazu said, as if reading Kohtake's mind.

'Give it to me?'

'Uh-huh.'

'A letter?'

'Fusagi said it was something he never managed to give you.'

Kohtake was silent. Then she replied matter-of-factly, 'I see . . .'

Uncertainty swept across Kazu's face. Kohtake's reaction to this news was unexpectedly cool. Was it impertinent to have mentioned it?

But Kohtake's response wasn't anything to do with Kazu. The real reason for her curt response was the fact that Fusagi's having written her a letter didn't make much sense. After all, he was never any good at reading or writing.

Fusagi had grown up poor in a small derelict town. His family was in the seaweed trade and every member helped out. But helping out affected his schoolwork so badly that he never learned to write anything more than hiragana, and a hundred or so kanji characters – roughly what a child normally learns in the first years of elementary school.

Kohtake and Fusagi were introduced to each other via a mutual acquaintance. Kohtake was twenty-one while Fusagi was twenty-six. This was before everyone had mobile phones, so they communicated by landline and letters. Fusagi wanted to be a landscape gardener, and lived wherever he worked. Kohtake had started nursing college, which further reduced their opportunities to meet. They did communicate, though – by letter.

Kohtake wrote all kinds of things in her letters. She wrote about herself, of course. She wrote about what went on at the nursing college, of good books she had read, and dreams of the future. She wrote of events which ranged from the mundane to the major news of the day, explaining in detail her feelings and reactions. Sometimes the letters were as long as ten pages.

Fusagi's replies, on the other hand, were always short. There were even times when he would send one-line replies like, 'Thanks for the interesting letter,' or, 'I know just what you mean.' At first, Kohtake thought he must be busy with work and didn't have the time to reply, but in letter after letter Fusagi continued to give these brief replies. She took this to mean that he wasn't very interested in her. Kohtake wrote in her letter that if he wasn't interested then he shouldn't bother replying, that with this letter she would stop writing if she didn't get a reply.

Fusagi normally replied within a week, but not this time. There was still nothing after a month. This was a shock to Kohtake. Certainly, his replies were short. But they never sounded negative, like they had been written out of obliga- tion. On the contrary, they always seemed frank and genuine. So she wouldn't give up quite yet. In fact, she was still waiting two and a half months after she had sent the ultimatum.

Then one day, after those two months, a letter arrived from Fusagi. All it said was: 'Let's get married.'

Those few words managed to move her in a way she had never felt before. But Kohtake found it hard to reply properly to such a letter, Fusagi having opened his heart in such a way. In the end, she simply wrote:

'Yes, let's.'

It wasn't until later that she learned he could barely read or write. When she found out, she asked him how he managed to read all the long letters she wrote to him. Apparently, he just allowed his eyes to wander over them. Then he just wrote in his reply the vague impression he got from this gazing. But with the last letter, after casting his eyes over it, he was over- come with a feeling that he had missed something important. He read it word by word while asking different people to tell him what the words were – hence the long time it took to reply.

Kohtake still looked like she couldn't believe it.

'It was a brown envelope, about this size,' said Kazu drawing in the air with her fingers.

'A brown envelope?'

Using a brown envelope for a letter sounded like something Fusagi would do, but it still didn't make sense to Kohtake.

'A love letter perhaps?' suggested Kei, her eyes sparkling innocently.

Kohtake smiled wryly. 'No, not a chance,' she said, dismissing the idea with a wave of her hands.

'But if it was a love letter, what will you do?' Kazu asked with an awkward smile.

She didn't normally pry into people's private lives, but perhaps she was running with the idea it was a love letter to help get rid of the dark mood that had until then hung in the air.

Also eager to change the subject, Kohtake willingly accepted the love-letter theory proposed by those who were unaware of how awful Fusagi was at reading and writing. 'I suppose I would want to read it,' she replied with a grin.

That was no lie. If he had written her a love letter, of course she wanted to read it.

'Why not go back and see?' Kei said.

'What?' Kohtake looked at Kei, her face blank with incomprehension.

Kazu responded to Kei's crazy idea by hurriedly placing her glass on the counter. 'Sis, seriously?' she said, bringing her face close to Kei's.

'She should read it,' Kei said, assertively.

'Kei, my love, hold on,' Kohtake said, trying hard to slow her down, but it was already too late.

Kei was breathing heavily and was not interested in Kohtake's effort to restrain her. 'If it's a love letter that Fusagi wrote to you, you need to receive it!'

Kei was convinced it was a love letter. And as long as she had this in her mind, she wouldn't be stopped. Kohtake had known her long enough to realize that.

Kazu didn't look like she was particularly comfortable with where this was going, but she just sighed and smiled.

Kohtake once again looked at the seat vacated by the woman in the dress. She had heard the rumour about returning to the past. She also knew about the various frustrating rules, and never – not once – had she ever contemplated going back in time herself. She was even uncertain as to whether the rumour was true. But if, say, it was true, she was now definitely interested in trying it. She wanted, more than anything, to know what the letter contained. If what Kazu said was right, if she was able to return to the day that Fusagi had planned to give it to her, she saw a glimmer of hope that she might still get to read it.

She had, however, a dilemma. Now that she knew Fusagi wanted to go back in time to give her a letter, was it right to go back to the past to receive it? She was in two minds – it seemed wrong to get hold of the letter that way. She took a deep breath and took stock of the current situation calmly.

She remembered the rule that going back in time would not change the present, no matter how much you tried. That meant that even if she returned to the past and read that letter, nothing would change.

'It won't change,' Kazu said, bluntly, when Kohtake asked to double check.

Kohtake felt something large stirring in her heart. So, no change to the present meant that even if she went back and took it, Fusagi would, in the present, still be intending to return to the past to give her the letter.

She gulped down her glass of Seven Happinesses. It was just the thing to set her resolve. Exhaling deeply, she put the glass down on the counter. 'That's right. That's right,' she muttered to herself. 'If it's really a love letter written for me, how can it be a problem if I read it?'

Calling it a *love letter* dispelled her feelings of guilt.

Kei nodded vigorously in agreement, and gulped down the orange juice as if to express solidarity with her. Her nostrils flared excitedly.

Kazu did not join the other two in downing her drink. She quietly placed the glass on the counter and disappeared into the kitchen.

Kohtake stood in front of the seat that would transport her. Feeling her blood pumping through her body, she carefully squeezed in between the chair and the table and sat down. The cafe's chairs all looked like antiques, elegantly shaped with cabriole legs. The seat and back were upholstered in a moss-green fabric, and Kohtake suddenly saw them in a fresh light. She noticed that all the chairs were in excellent condition as if they were brand new. It wasn't just the chairs, either; the entire cafe was sparkling clean. If this cafe opened at the beginning of the Meiji period, it must have been operating for more than a hundred years. Yet there was not the slightest hint of mustiness.

She sighed in admiration. She knew that in order to keep this cafe looking this way, someone must be spending a lot of time each day cleaning. She looked to her side to see standing there Kazu, who had approached without Kohtake noticing her. Standing there so quietly, there was something eerie about her appearance. She was carrying a silver tray, on which there were a white coffee cup and, instead of the glass carafe normally used to serve customers, a small silver kettle.

Kohtake's heart skipped a beat as she saw how stunning Kazu looked. Her normal girlish qualities had disappeared, and she now wore an expression that was both elegant and intimidatingly sombre.

'You're familiar with the rules, right?' Kazu asked in a casual but distant tone.

Kohtake hurriedly went through the rules in her mind.

The first rule was that when returning to the past, the only people one could meet were those who had visited the cafe.

That's no problem for me, thought Kohtake. *Fusagi has visited here countless times.*

The second rule was that the present wouldn't be changed by returning to the past, no matter how hard one tried. Kohtake had already reassured herself that this rule wasn't a problem. Of course, this did not only apply to letters. If, for example, a revolutionary treatment for Alzheimer's disease was discovered and somehow taken back to the past to be tried on Fusagi, it would be unable to improve his condition.

It seemed an unkind rule.

The third rule was that, in order to return to the past, one had to sit in this seat in particular. By chance, the woman in the dress had gone to the toilet just at that moment. The narrow window of opportunity was perfectly timed for Kohtake to take advantage of. She had also heard – though didn't know if it was true – that if you tried to forcefully remove the woman in the dress from her seat, she would curse you. So coincidence or not, Kohtake felt lucky indeed.

But the rules did not end there.

The fourth rule was that when one returned to the past, it was not possible to move from the chair in which one was seated. It wasn't that you were stuck to the chair, but rather that if you did get up, you would be forcefully brought back to the present. As this cafe was in a basement, there was no mobile-phone signal, hence there was no chance of going back and calling someone who wasn't there. Also, not being able to leave your seat meant you couldn't go outside – yet another detestable rule.

Kohtake had heard that several years ago the cafe had become quite famous, attracting a throng of customers who all wanted to return to the past. *With all these maddening rules, no wonder people stopped coming*, she thought.

Kohtake suddenly realized that Kazu was silently waiting for her reply. 'I have to drink the coffee before it goes cold, right?'

'Yes.'

'Is there anything else?'

There was one other thing she wanted to know: *how could she make sure that she returned to the right day and time?*

'You need to form a strong image of the day you want to return to,' Kazu added, as if reading her mind.

Simply being asked to form an image was rather vague. 'An image?' Kohtake asked.

'A day before Fusagi forgot you. A day when he was thinking of passing you the letter . . . and a day when he brought the letter with him to the cafe.'

A day when he still remembered her – it was a rough guess, but she remembered a day in summer three years ago. It was a time before Fusagi had shown any symptoms.

A day when he meant to hand her the letter – this was difficult. If she hadn't received it, how could she know? Yet it would be meaningless to return to a day before he'd written the letter. She decided she should simply visualize an image of Fusagi writing to her.

And a day when he brought the letter with him to the cafe – this one was important. Even if she managed to go back in time and meet him, if he didn't have the letter, everything would become pointless. Luckily, she knew that he normally put all his important things in his black zippered portfolio, and he would carry this with him. If it was a love letter, he wouldn't leave it lying around at home. He would definitely be carrying it with him in his zippered portfolio so that she wouldn't happen upon it.

She didn't know the day when he meant to give it to her, but where there was a bag, there was a way. She formed an image of Fusagi carrying his zippered portfolio with him.

'Are you ready?' said Kazu in a calm, quiet voice.

'Just a moment.' She took a deep breath. She formed the images one more time. 'Day he doesn't forget . . . letter . . . day he came . . .' she chanted softly.

OK, enough messing around.

'I'm ready,' she said, staring directly into Kazu's eyes.

Kazu gave a small nod. She set the empty coffee cup in front of Kohtake and carefully picked up the silver kettle from the tray in her right hand. Her ballerina-like motions were efficient and beautiful.

'Just remember . . .' Kazu paused, facing Kohtake with downcast eyes. 'Drink the coffee before it goes cold.'

These soft words echoed through the silent cafe. Kohtake sensed how tense the atmosphere had become.

With a serious and ceremonial air, Kazu began pouring coffee into the cup.

A thin stream of pitch-black coffee poured from the narrow spout of the silver kettle. Unlike the gurgling sound made by coffee poured from a carafe with a wide mouth, the coffee filled the white coffee cup silently and ever so slowly.

Kohtake had never seen such a kettle before. It was a little smaller than those she had seen at other cafes. Solidly built, it looked very elegant and refined. *The coffee is probably special as well*, she thought.

As such thoughts were passing through her mind, a wisp of steam rose from the now-full cup. At that moment, everything around Kohtake began to ripple and shimmer. Her entire field of vision suddenly seemed surreal. She recalled the glass of Seven Happinesses she recently downed. *Perhaps I'm feeling its effects?*

No. This was definitely different. What she was experiencing was far more alarming. Her body had also begun rippling and shimmering. She had become the steam coming off the coffee. It seemed as if everything around her was unravelling.

Kohtake closed her eyes, not out of fear, but in an attempt to focus. If indeed she was now travelling back in time, she wanted to mentally prepare herself.

The very first time Kohtake noticed a change in Fusagi, it was because of something he said. On the day he admitted out loud what had happened, Kohtake was preparing dinner while waiting for him to come home. A landscape gardener's work does not simply involve pruning branches and raking leaves. He has to consider the balance between the house and the garden. The garden cannot be too colourful, nor can it be too plain. 'The keyword is balance.' That was what Fusagi had always said. His work day began early but finished at dusk. Unless there was a particular reason not to, Fusagi would come home straight away. So when Kohtake didn't have a night shift, she would wait for him and they would eat together.

On this occasion, night came, but Fusagi had still not come home. This was unusual behaviour, but Kohtake assumed he must have gone out drinking with colleagues.

When, finally, he did come home, it was two hours later than usual. Normally, when he came home he would always ring the doorbell three times. But that night, he didn't ring. Instead, Kohtake heard the sound of the door knob turning and a voice from outside saying, 'It's me.'

On hearing his voice, she rushed and opened the door in a panic. She thought he must have hurt himself in some way that prevented him from ringing the doorbell. But there he was, looking as he always did: dressed simply in his grey gardening smock with his navy breeches. He had taken his tool bag from his shoulder, and, looking a little ashamed of himself, admitted, 'I got lost.'

That had happened around the end of summer two years ago.

Being a nurse, Kohtake had been trained to recognize early symptoms of a whole range of illnesses. This was more than simply forgetting something. She was sure of it. Soon after he began to forget whether or not he had done a task at work. After the illness had progressed a bit further, he would wake in the night and say out loud, 'I forgot to do something important.' When this happened, she wouldn't argue with him; she focused on calming him and reassuring him that they could check up on it in the morning.

She even consulted a doctor behind his back. She was keen to try anything that might slow the advancement of his disease, even if by just a little.

But as the days went on, he began to forget more and more.

He liked to travel. It wasn't the travel itself that he liked, but the opportunity to visit gardens in different places. Kohtake always arranged to take her holidays at the same time as him so that they could go together. He would complain and say he was going for work, but that didn't bother her. While on a trip, his brow seemed permanently furrowed, but she knew that this was how he looked whenever he was doing something he liked.

Even as his illness progressed, he didn't stop travelling, but he did start visiting the same destination over and over again.

After a while the illness began to affect their daily lives. He often forgot that he had bought things. More and more often, there would be days when he would ask, 'Who bought this?' and then spend the rest of the day in a bad mood. They lived in the apartment they had moved to after getting married, but he began not coming home and she would frequently get calls from the police. Then about six months ago, he started calling her by her maiden name, Kohtake.

Finally the dizzy sensation of rippling and shimmering faded. Kohtake opened her eyes. She saw the slowly rotating ceiling fan . . . her hands, and her feet. She was no longer steam.

However, she didn't know whether she had actually gone back in time. The cafe had no windows and the lighting was always dim. Unless one looked at a watch, there was no way of knowing whether it was day or night. The three solid-looking clocks on the wall all showed completely different times.

But something was different. Kazu had vanished. Kei was nowhere to be seen either. Kohtake tried to calm herself, but she was unable to stop her heart from beating faster and faster. She once again looked around the cafe.

'There's no one here,' she muttered. The absence of Fus-agi, who she had gone back to meet, was a huge disappointment.

She looked at the ceiling fan in a daze and considered her plight.

It was a shame, but perhaps it was for the best. Actually, in some ways she was relieved. Of course she wanted to read the letter. But she couldn't help feeling guilty that she was sneaking a peek, so to speak. Fusagi would have surely been cross to learn that she had come from the future to read what he had written.

It wasn't as if anything she did would change the present anyway. It didn't matter if she never read it. If by reading it his condition would somehow improve, then of course she would – she would give her life for that. But the letter had nothing to do with his condition. It wouldn't change the fact that he had forgotten her, either.

She coolly and rationally considered her predicament. Just earlier, she had the shock of him asking her whether they'd met before. It had really upset her. She had known this time would come, but it still caught her off balance, and brought her here.

She was beginning to feel more composed.

If this was the past, then it held nothing of use. *I should return to the present. Even if I am just a stranger to Fusagi, I can be his nurse. I must do what I can.* She remembered her heart's resolve and reaffirmed it.

'I doubt it's a love letter,' she muttered to herself as she reached out for the cup of coffee.

CLANG-DONG

Someone had entered the cafe. To enter this cafe, one has to descend stairs from the ground level, and go in through a large door about two metres high, made out of solid wood. It's when this door opens that the bell sounds, but the visitor does not immediately appear at the entrance, as a small patch of flooring must be crossed first. Once the bell rings, there is a time lag of a few seconds before the visitor takes those one or two steps and enters the cafe.

So when the bell rang, Kohtake had no idea who had come in. *Was it Nagare? Or Kei?* She noticed how nervous the suspense was making her. Her heart was racing in excitement. It wasn't the kind of thing she normally did – a once in a lifetime experience, to be exact. *If it was Kei, she would probably ask me why. Kazu, on the other hand, would just probably deliver her usual customer service . . . that would probably be a disappointment.*

Kohtake played out various scenarios in her mind. But the person who appeared was neither Kei nor Kazu. Standing in the doorway was Fusagi.

'Oh . . .' Kohtake said. His sudden appearance had taken her by surprise. It was him she had come back to see, but she hadn't been expecting him to walk into the cafe right then.

He was wearing a navy polo shirt and beige knee-length shorts. It was what he often wore on his days off. It must have been hot outside, as he was fanning himself with his black zippered portfolio.

She sat unmoving in her chair. He stood at the entrance for a while, staring at her with an odd look.

'Hi there,' she began.

She felt clueless as to how she was going to broach what she had come to talk about. He had never stared at her like this. Not since they met – let alone since they had been married. It was both flattering and embarrassing.

She had formed a hazy image of three years ago but she didn't know how to make sure that that was where she was.

Maybe she hadn't imagined it right, and if that was the case, what was to say that by some mistake she'd got the *three* right, but she had only returned to *three days* ago? Just when she began to think she might have been too vague . . .

'Oh hello. I didn't expect to see you here,' he said matter-of-factly.

Fusagi sounded like he had before he became ill. He was as she had pictured him – that is to say, he was how she remembered him.

'I was waiting, but you didn't come home,' he added.

He looked away from her gaze. He coughed nervously with a furrowed brow, as if uncomfortable with something.

'So it's really you?' she said.

'Huh?'

'You know who I am?'

'What?' He looked at her with bemusement.

But she was, of course, not joking. She had to make sure. It was obvious that she had returned to the past. But when? Before or after the onset of the Alzheimer's?

'Just say my name,' she said.

'Are you going to stop messing with me?' he spat out crossly.

Though he hadn't answered the question, she smiled with relief. 'No, it's OK,' she said, shaking her head a little.

This short exchange told her everything she needed to know. She had definitely gone back. The Fusagi standing before her was Fusagi from before he had lost his memory. And if the image she pictured had worked, it was the Fusagi of three years ago. Kohtake smiled as she gave her coffee an unnecessary stir.

Fusagi observed Kohtake and her peculiar behaviour. 'You're acting a bit strange today,' he said, looking around the cafe, as if he had just realized no one else was there.

'Nagare, you here?' he called to the kitchen.

With no reply, he went behind the counter, flapping his *setta* sandals as he walked. He peeked into the back room, but no one was there.

'That's odd. No one's here,' he grumbled. He sat down on the counter seat furthest away from Kohtake.

She coughed on purpose to get his attention. He looked at her, fed up.

'What is it?'

'Why are you sitting there?'

'Why not? What's stopping me?'

'Why not come and sit here?'

She rapped on the table to beckon him to sit in the empty seat facing her. But he winced at the idea.

'No. I'm fine,' he replied.

'Oh, come on now . . . Why not?'

'A mature married couple, sitting down together like that . . . nah,' Fusagi said, a little crossly. The crevice between his brows deepened. He was dismissive of the idea, but when his brow furrowed in that way, it wasn't that he was displeased. On the contrary, it was a sign that he was in a good mood.

She knew all too well it was meant to conceal his embarrassment.

'True. We're a married couple,' she agreed, smiling. She was so happy to hear the word *couple* from his lips.

'Ugh . . . Don't be so sentimental . . .'

Now anything he said brought back waves of nostalgia . . . and happiness. She absent-mindedly sipped the coffee.

'Uh-oh,' she said out loud, as she realized how much the coffee had cooled. It suddenly dawned on her how limited her time there was. She had to do what she had to do before it went completely cold.

'Look, there's something I need to ask you.'

'What? What is it?'

'Is there anything . . . anything you want to hand me?'

Kohtake's heart started racing. Fusagi had written it before the onset of his illness, it *may* have been a love letter. *Totally impossible* . . . she was telling herself. *But if it were* . . . Her wish to read it was now running wild, reassured by the fact that no matter what she did, the present would not change.

'What?'

'About this by this . . .'

She drew the size of the envelope in the air using her fingers, just as Kazu had shown her. Her direct approach provoked alarm in his face, as he glared at her, completely motionless. *I've blown it*, she thought on seeing his expression. She remembered that something similar had happened soon after they were married.

Fusagi had a present ready to give her for her birthday. On the day before, by accident, she saw it among his belongings. Never before having received a present from him, she was overjoyed at the prospect of receiving this first gift. On the day of her birthday, when he had returned home from work, she was so excited that she asked him, 'Don't you have something special for me today?' But on hearing this, he went very quiet. 'No, nothing in particular,' he said. The next day, she found her present in the bin. It was the lilac handkerchief.

She felt she had repeated the same mistake. He hated being told to do something that he had been meaning to do himself. Now she feared that even if he was carrying the letter, he would never give it to her – especially if it was a love letter. She regretted her carelessness even more so because time was of the essence. He still looked alarmed. She smiled at him.

'I'm so sorry. I didn't mean anything. Please forget it,' she said in a light-hearted way. Then to emphasize that it didn't really matter to her either way, she tried to make small talk. 'Hey, I just thought: why don't we do *sukiyaki* tonight?'

It was his favourite dish. He seemed to be in a sulky mood, but this usually lifted his spirits.

She slowly reached for the cup and felt the temperature of the coffee with her palm. It was still OK. She still had time. She could cherish these precious moments with him. She wanted to forget the letter for the time being. Judging by his reaction, he definitely had written her something. If he hadn't, he would have responded in no uncertain terms, 'What on earth are you talking about?' If she allowed the current situation to play out, he would end up throwing the letter away. She decided to change strategy. She would try to alter his mood to prevent a repeat of what happened on her birthday.

She looked at him. His face was still serious. But then again, it was always like that. He never wanted her to think that just by hearing *sukiyaki* his mood instantly lifted. He wasn't that straightforward. This was Fusagi before Alzheimer's. Even his sulky face was precious to her. It was bliss to be with him again now. But she had read the situation wrongly.

'Oh, I get it. I see what's happening,' he said, with a gloomy look. He got up from the counter and walked over to stand in front of her.

'What do you mean?' she asked, looking up at him. He was striking an imposing stance as he glared back at her. 'What's wrong?' She hadn't seen him like this before.

'You're from the future . . . aren't you?'

'What?'

What he had just said could be considered crazy. But he was right – she had come from the future.

'Er. Now, look . . .' She was racking her brains trying to remember whether there was a rule that said, *When you go back in time, you cannot reveal that you are from the future.* But none existed.

'Look, I can explain—'

'I thought it was strange that you were sitting in that seat.'

'Yes . . . well.'

'So that means you know about my illness.'

She felt her heart start racing again. She thought she had been transported back to a time before his disease – but she was wrong. The Fusagi standing before her knew he was ill.

Just from looking at his clothes, she could tell it was summertime. She had been transported back to the summer of two years ago – the time when he began losing his way, when she began noticing the telltale signs of his illness. If she had gone back by as little as a year, her conversation with him would have become muddled by now.

Rather than three years ago, she had returned to the day that met with the criteria she had imagined: *a day when Fusagi had not forgotten her . . . a day when he was thinking of passing*

her the letter . . . and a day when he brought it with him to the cafe.
To have gone back three years would have meant that he had
not yet written the letter.

The Fusagi standing before her knew he was ill, and so it
was likely that the content of the letter concerned his disease.
Also, the way he reacted with such dread when she mentioned
the letter seemed further evidence.

'You know, don't you?' he said forcefully, pressing her to
give an answer. She couldn't see how she could lie at this stage.
She nodded silently.

'I see,' he muttered.

She regained her composure. *OK, whatever I do here, it's not
going to change the present. But it might upset him . . . I never
would have returned to the past if I thought that might happen.
How embarrassing that I was all caught up in the idea of it being
a love letter.*

She felt deep, deep regret for coming back. But now was
not the time to be wallowing. He had gone silent.

'My love?' she called out to the despondent-looking Fusagi.

She had never seen him looking so depressed. It was heart-
wrenching. He suddenly turned his back on her and walked
back towards the counter where he had been sitting. He picked
up the black portfolio. From it, he pulled a brown envelope
and walked back to her. His face showed no signs of wretched-
ness or desperation; he looked more embarrassed than anything else.

He began to mumble in a throaty voice that was difficult
to hear.

'The "you" living in this time doesn't know about my
illness . . .'

He might be under that impression. But 'I' already know, or will very soon.

'I just don't know how to tell you . . .'

He held up the brown envelope to show her. He was planning to tell her that he had Alzheimer's in this letter.

But I don't need to read it . . . I already know. It would make more sense to give it to me in the past. The 'me' that Fusagi can't bring himself to give it to . . . I guess if he can't pass it to that version of me, it's OK that I take it. That's just the way things are.

She decided to leave while things were as they were at that moment. She didn't want the subject of his illness to be broached. The worst-case scenario was him asking about his condition in the present. If he asked how his condition progressed, who knows how he would take the awful news. She should return before he asked. Now was the time to return to the present . . .

The coffee was now at a temperature that she could down it in one go.

'I can't let the coffee go cold,' she said and brought the cup close to her mouth.

'So I forget? I forget you?' he mumbled, looking down.

Hearing this, she was overwhelmed by confusion. She didn't even know why there was a coffee cup in front of her.

She looked at him in trepidation. Staring at him, she noticed how forlorn his expression was now. She had never imagined that he could look that way. Lost for words, she couldn't even maintain eye contact and found herself casting her eyes down.

By giving no reply, she had answered his question with a yes.

'I see. I feared as much,' he murmured sadly. He bowed his head so deeply his neck looked like it might break.

Her eyes welled with tears. After being diagnosed with Alzheimer's, he had struggled each day with the dread and anxiety of losing his memory. Yet she, his wife, had not seen how he had borne these thoughts and feelings alone. On learning that she had come from the future, the first thing he had wanted to know was whether he had forgotten her, his wife. This realization filled her with both joy and sorrow.

It gave her the strength to look him in the face, without wiping away her tears. She smiled broadly at him so he might interpret her tears as those of joy.

'Actually, your illness does get better, you know.'

(*As a nurse, now is the time I need to be strong.*)

'In fact, you in the future told me.'

(*I can say anything without changing the present.*)

'How you did have anxious moments . . .'

(What does it hurt if I lie? If I can relieve his anxiety, even if it's just for a moment, it's worth it . . .)

She wanted so much for her lie to be believed, she would do anything. She had a lump in her throat. Tears streamed down her face. But maintaining her beaming smile, she continued.

'It will be all right.'

(*It will be all right!*)

'You recover.'

(*You recover!*)

'Don't worry.'

(You recover . . . Really!)

Every word she spoke, she delivered with all her strength.

In her mind, it wasn't a lie. Even if he had forgotten who she was . . . Even if nothing she did changed the present. He looked her straight in the eyes and she looked right back at him, her face streaming with tears.

He looked happy. 'Oh really?' he said in a soft whisper.

'Yes,' she said.

He looked at her in the gentlest of ways. Looking down at the brown envelope he was holding in his hands, he slowly approached her. The distance between them was now such that a letter might be handed from one to the other.

'Here,' he said. Like a shy child, he offered her the brown envelope he was holding.

She tried to push the letter away. 'But you get better,' she said.

'Then you can throw it out,' he said, handing her the letter more forcefully. His tone was different from his normal gruff self. He spoke with such gentleness that it gave her the odd feeling that she must have missed something.

He once again pressed the brown envelope on her. Her trembling hands reached out and nervously took it. She wasn't really sure of his intentions.

'Drink up. Your coffee will go cold,' he said, acknowledging the rules. The kindness in his smile seemed infinite.

She nodded. It was just a small nod. With no words left, she reached for the coffee.

Once she had her hands firmly on the cup, he turned his back.

It was as if their time as a couple had reached its end. A large tear began to form in her eye.

'My love,' she cried out without thinking. He did not turn

round. His shoulders appeared to be trembling ever so slightly. While watching his back, she drank the coffee in one go. She drank it in one gulp, not out of a sense of urgency that the coffee was about to go cold, but rather out of respect for Fusagi, whose gentle back was turned to ensure she could quickly and safely return to the present. Such was the depth of his kindness.

'My darling.'

She felt overcome by a shimmering and rippling sensation. She returned the cup to its saucer. As her hand drew back, it seemed to dissolve into steam. All that was left to do was to return to the present. This fleeting moment, when they had once more been together as husband and wife, had ended.

Suddenly, he turned round – a reaction, perhaps, to the sound of her cup hitting the saucer. She didn't know how he could make her out, but he seemed to be able to see her there. As her consciousness flickered and dissipated into the steam, she saw his lips move a little.

Unless she was mistaken, he seemed to be saying, 'Thank you.'

Her consciousness had merged with the steam, and she had begun the transition from past to present. The cafe around her began to fast-forward. She could do nothing to stem the flow of her tears. In a blink, she realized Kazu and Kei had reappeared in her field of vision. She had returned to the present – the day that he had completely forgotten her. One look at her expression was enough to fill Kei's face with worry.

'The letter?' she asked. *Letter*, not *love letter*.

She dropped her gaze to the brown envelope she'd been

given by Fusagi in the past. She slowly removed the letter from the envelope.

It was written in basic script, all squiggly like crawling worms. It was definitely Fusagi's handwriting. As Kohtake read the letter, she held her right hand to her mouth to stop the sobbing as her tears fell.

So sudden was her outburst of tears that Kazu was worried. 'Kohtake . . . are you OK?' she asked.

Kohtake's shoulders began to shudder, and gradually she began wailing, louder and louder. Kazu and Kei stood there looking at her, unsure of what to do. After a while, she handed Kazu the letter.

Kazu took the letter, and, as if looking for permission, she looked at Kei behind the counter. Kei nodded slightly with a grave expression.

Kazu looked back at the tearful Kohtake and then began to read out loud.

> You're a nurse, so I can only assume you have already noticed. I have an illness where I forget things.
>
> I imagine that as I keep on losing my memory, you will be able to put aside your own feelings and care for me with the detachment of a nurse, and that you can do that no matter what strange things I say or do – even if I forget who you are.
>
> So I ask you never to forget one thing. You are my wife, and if life becomes too hard for you as my wife, I want you to leave me.
>
> You don't have to stay by me as a nurse. If I am no good as a husband, then I want you to leave me. All I ask

is that you can do what you can as my wife. We are husband and wife after all. Even if I lose my memory, I want to be together as husband and wife. I cannot stand the idea of us staying together only out of sympathy.

This is something I cannot say to your face, so I wrote it in a letter.

When Kazu finished reading, Kohtake and Kei looked up at the ceiling and began to cry loudly. Kohtake understood why Fusagi had handed this letter to her, his wife from the future. From the letter, it was clear that he had guessed what she would do after she found out about his illness. And then, when he came from the future, it became clear to him that, just as he predicted, in the future she was caring for him like a nurse.

Amid the anxiety and fear of losing his memory, he was hoping that she would continue to be his wife. She was always in his heart.

There was more proof of this to be found. Even after losing his memory, he could content himself by looking at travel magazines, opening his notebook, and jotting something down. She had once looked at what he wrote. He had been listing the destinations that he had travelled to in order to visit gardens. She had simply assumed his actions were a hangover from his love of his work as a landscape gardener. But she was wrong. The destinations he made a note of were all the places that he had visited with her. She didn't notice at the time. She couldn't see. These notes were the last hand-hold for Fusagi, who was gradually forgetting who she was.

Of course, that she had looked after him as a nurse didn't feel like a mistake to her. She had believed that it was for the best. And he didn't write the letter to blame her in any way either. It seemed to her that he knew that her talk about him getting *healed* was a lie, but it was a lie he wanted to believe. *Otherwise*, she thought, *he wouldn't have said 'thank you'.*

After her crying had stopped, the woman in the dress returned from the toilet, stood in front of her and spoke just one word.

'Move!' she said in a low voice.

'Sure,' she said, leaping up and relinquishing the seat.

The woman in the dress's reappearance was impeccably timed, coinciding with a switch in Kohtake's mood. Eyes swollen from crying, she looked at Kazu and Kei. She held up the letter that Kazu had just read, and waved it.

'So there you have it,' she said with a grin.

Kei responded by nodding, her round bright eyes still streaming tears like a waterfall.

'What have I been doing?' Kohtake mumbled, looking at the letter.

'Kohtake,' Kei sniffled, looking worried.

Kohtake neatly folded the letter and returned it to the envelope. 'I'm going home,' she said, in a bold, confident voice.

Kazu gave a small nod. Kei was still sniffing. Kohtake looked at the still-teary Kei, who had cried longer than she had. She smiled as she thought that Kei must be getting pretty dehydrated, and let out a deep breath. No longer looking lost, she seemed empowered. She pulled out her purse from her shoulder bag on the counter and handed Kazu 380 yen in coins.

'Thanks,' she said.

With a calm expression, Kazu returned her smile.

Kohtake gave a quick nod and walked towards the entrance. She stepped lightly. She was in a hurry to see Fusagi's face.

She passed through the doorway and out of sight.

'Ah!' she said and doubled back into the cafe. Kazu and Kei looked at her enquiringly.

'One more thing,' she said. 'Starting tomorrow, no more calling me by my maiden name, OK?'

She grinned broadly.

It was Kohtake who originally requested that she be called by her maiden name. When Fusagi had started calling her Kohtake, she wanted to avoid confusion. But such consideration was not necessary now. A smile returned to Kei's face and her bright eyes opened widely.

'OK, got you,' she said happily.

'Tell everyone else too,' said Kohtake, and without waiting for a reply, she waved and left.

CLANG-DONG

'OK,' said Kazu, as if speaking to herself, and put the money from Kohtake in the till.

Kei cleaned away the cup that Kohtake had drunk from and went into the kitchen to get a refill for the woman in the dress. The *clank, clank* sound of the keys of the cash register reverberated through the cool room. The ceiling fan continued to rotate silently. Kei returned and poured a new coffee for the woman in the dress. 'We appreciate your presence again this summer,' she whispered.

The woman in the dress continued to read her novel and did not reply. Kei placed her hand on her own stomach and smiled.

Summer was just getting started.

III

The Sisters

A girl was sitting quietly in *that* seat.

She looked old enough to be in high school. She had large, sweet eyes. She was wearing a beige turtleneck with a tartan-check miniskirt, black tights, and moss-brown boots. A duffel coat hung on the back of her chair. Her clothes could have been worn by an adult but there was something childlike about her expression. Her hair was cut in a bob to her jawline. She wore no make-up but her naturally long eyelashes accentuated her pretty features. Although she came from the future, there was nothing that would have prevented her from passing in public as someone from the present – if it hadn't been for that rule that said that anyone visiting from the future must stay in *that* seat. As it was early August, her clothes would, however, have looked terribly out of season.

It was still a mystery as to who she had come to meet. Right now, the only person in the cafe was Nagare Tokita. The large-framed man with narrow eyes was wearing a cook's uniform and standing behind the counter.

But the cafe proprietor didn't seem to be who the girl had come to meet. Although her eyes were looking at Nagare, they showed no sign of emotion towards him. She seemed to be totally indifferent to his existence. But at the same time, no one else was in the cafe. Nagare stood there looking at her with his arms crossed.

Nagare was a large man. Any ordinary girl, or woman for that matter, might have felt a little threatened sitting in that small cafe alone with him. But the untroubled expression on this girl's face suggested that she couldn't care less.

The girl and Nagare had exchanged no words. The girl had been doing nothing except occasionally glancing at one of the clocks on the wall, as if she was worried about the time.

Suddenly Nagare's nose twitched and his right eye opened wider. A *ching* from the toaster in the kitchen rang out. Food was ready. He went into the kitchen and began busily preparing something. The girl didn't pay any attention to the noise and took a sip of her coffee. She nodded as if to say *yes*. The coffee must have still been warm as her expression suggested that she had plenty of time. Nagare came out from the kitchen. He was carrying a rectangular tray with toast and butter, salad, and fruit yogurt on it. The butter was home-made – his speciality. His butter was so good that the woman in curlers, Yaeko Hirai, would come in for some, armed with a plastic container.

Nagare got a lot of joy from watching the customers' delight as they ate his delicious butter. The problem was that although he used the most expensive ingredients, the butter was free for customers. He didn't charge for condiments; he was very particular about that. These high standards of his were quite a problem.

Still holding the tray, he stood in front of the girl. His large frame must have seemed like a giant wall to the petite girl seated there.

He looked down at her. 'Who did you come to meet?' he asked, getting straight to the point.

The girl looked up at the giant wall standing there. She casually stared at him. He was used to his huge size causing surprise and apprehension in those who didn't know him; it felt strange now that he didn't have this effect.

'What?' he asked.

But the girl didn't offer much of a response.

'No one in particular,' she just said and took another sip of coffee. She wouldn't engage with him at all.

Tilting his head to one side, he gracefully placed the tray on the table for the girl and then returned to his place behind the counter. The girl looked uncomfortable.

'Uh, excuse me,' she called to Nagare.

'What?'

'I didn't order this,' the girl said awkwardly, pointing to the toast in front of her.

'On the house,' he said with pride.

The girl looked at all the free food with disbelief. He uncrossed his arms and leaned forward with both hands on the counter.

'You made all the effort to come from the future. I can't have a girl like you going back without serving you anything,' he said, perhaps expecting at least a *thank you*. But the girl just kept staring at him and didn't even smile. He felt obliged to respond.

'Is there a problem?' he said, a bit rattled.

'No. Thank you, I'll eat it.'

'Attagirl.'

'Well, why wouldn't I?'

The girl expertly spread the butter on the toast and took a hungry mouthful. She kept on munching. She had a wonderful way of eating.

He was waiting for the girl's reaction. Naturally, he thought, she would show her delight upon eating his boast-worthy butter. But she did not react as he had anticipated – she carried on eating without changing her expression. When she finished the toast, she started crunching on the salad and gobbling down the fruit yogurt.

On finishing, the girl just folded her hands in thanks for the food without having made a single comment. Nagare was crestfallen.

CLANG-DONG

It was Kazu. She handed the key ring with its wad of keys to Nagare behind the counter.

'I'm ba—' she said, stopping mid-word when she noticed the girl in *that* seat.

'Hey,' replied Nagare, pocketing the key ring. He didn't say, '*Hey, welcome back,*' like he normally would.

Kazu grabbed his wrist, and whispered: 'Who's she?'

'I've been trying to find out,' he replied.

Normally Kazu wouldn't particularly pay much attention to who was sitting there. When someone appeared, she could easily tell that the person had come from the future to meet someone. It was not something she interfered in.

But never had such a young, pretty girl sat in that chair before. She couldn't help but openly stare at her.

Her staring did not go unnoticed.

'Hello!' said the girl, offering a pleasant smile.

Nagare's left eyebrow twitched in annoyance that she hadn't offered such a smile to him.

'Did you come to meet someone?' said Kazu.

'Yeah. I guess,' the girl conceded.

Hearing this conversation, Nagare tightened his lips. He had asked the same question just moments earlier and the girl had said no. He wasn't amused.

'But they're not here, are they?' he said crossly, turning away.

So who was she planning to meet? Kazu wondered as she tapped her index finger against her chin.

'Huh? Surely it wasn't him?' She pointed the chin-tapping finger towards Nagare.

Nagare pointed at himself. 'Me?' He folded his arms and muttered, 'Um, er . . .' as if he was trying to remember the circumstances surrounding the girl's appearance.

The girl had appeared on *that* seat about ten minutes ago. Kei had needed to go to the gynaecology clinic so Kazu had driven her there. Normally Nagare would take Kei to her regular check-ups, but today was different.

He considered the gynaecology clinic to be a sanctuary for

women only, *where no man should venture*. That was why he was manning the cafe alone.

(*Did she choose a time when only I was working?*)

His heart lifted at the thought.

(So perhaps the way she's been until now is down to her being embarrassed . . .)

Stroking his chin, he nodded as if it all made sense. He sprang from the counter and sat down in the chair facing the girl.

The girl stared back at him blankly.

He no longer looked like the person he had been until a moment ago.

If her coldness towards me is just out of shyness, I'll try to be more approachable, he thought and grinned broadly.

He leaned forward on his elbows in an easy-going way. 'So, was it me that you came to visit?' he asked the girl.

'No way.'

'Me? You came to meet me?'

'No.'

'Me?'

'No!'

'. . .'

The girl was adamant. Kazu heard the exchange and came to a simple conclusion.

'Well you're completely ruled out.'

Again, Nagare was deflated. 'OK . . . so it's not me,' he said sulkily as he trudged back to the counter.

The girl seemed to find this amusing and let out a cheeky giggle.

CLANG-DONG

When the bell rang, the girl looked at the clock in the middle of the wall. This clock in the middle was the only one that was accurate. The other two were either slow or fast. She must have known that. The girl's eyes were fixed on the entrance.

A moment later, Kei walked into the cafe.

'Thanks, Kazu, dear,' she said as she entered. She was wearing an aqua-coloured dress and strappy sandals, and was fanning herself with a straw hat. She had gone out with Kazu, but, judging from the plastic shopping bag she was holding, she must have popped into the convenience store nearby before coming into the cafe. Kei was, by nature, a carefree person. Always charming and never shy, she was comfortable with the most intimidating of customers; she would be friendly and outgoing, even when communicating with a foreigner who spoke no Japanese.

When Kei noticed the girl sitting in *that* seat, she said, 'Hello, welcome,' while wearing a big smile. Her smile was beaming even more than normal, and the tone of her voice was a little higher too.

The girl straightened in her chair and bowed her head a little, keeping her gaze on Kei.

Kei responded with a smile and trotted towards the back room.

'So how was it?' Nagare asked Kei.

Given where she and Kazu had just returned from, there could be only one thing that he wanted to know. Kei patted her still flat stomach, gave him the peace sign, and smiled.

'Ah. Right then,' he said.

He narrowed his eyes further and gave two small nods. When he felt joy, he found himself unable to express his happiness openly. Knowing this all too well, Kei looked on at his reaction with contentment.

With keenly observing eyes, the girl in *that* seat watched this exchange warmly. Kei didn't seem to notice how the girl was watching her and began walking to the back room.

As if this was some kind of cue, the girl called out in an unexpectedly loud voice. 'Excuse me?'

Kei stopped in her tracks and answered unthinkingly. 'Yes?' She turned and looked at the girl with her round, bright eyes.

The girl self-consciously averted her eyes and began fidgeting.

'What is it?' Kei asked.

The girl looked up as if she indeed wanted something; her smile was honest and sweet. The cool distance she expressed towards Nagare had vanished entirely.

'Um. It's just . . .'

'Yes? What is it?'

'I'd like to take my photo with you.'

Kei blinked, startled by the girl's words. 'With me?' she asked.

'Yes.'

Nagare immediately responded. 'With her?' he asked, pointing to Kei.

'Yes,' said the girl cheerily.

'Are you saying that you came to see her?' asked Kazu.

'Yes.'

Kei's eyes beamed brightly at this unknown girl's sudden

confession. Kei was never suspicious of strangers. So rather than asking the girl who she was or why she wanted the photo, she immediately said, 'Oh! Really? Can I fix my make-up first?'

She pulled out a case from her shoulder bag and began fixing her make-up.

'Um, there's no time,' the girl said urgently.

'Oh . . . No, of course.'

Naturally, Kei knew the rules well. Her cheeks flushed as she snapped the case shut.

The girl was prevented from positioning herself alongside Kei, as you would normally do when asking for a photo, by the rule prohibiting her to move from *that* seat. Kei passed her convenience-store plastic bag and straw hat to Kazu and stood next to the girl.

'Where's your camera?' asked Kazu.

The girl pushed something towards her across the table.

'Huh? Is that a camera?' asked Kei in surprise, as Kazu looked at the camera handed to her. It had the dimensions of a business card. Wafer-thin and semi-transparent, it just looked like a plastic card.

Kei was fascinated by it. She took a close look at it from all angles. 'It's so thin!'

'Um, we have to hurry. Time is almost up,' the girl said calmly to Kei.

'Yes, I'm sorry,' said Kei, shrugging her shoulders and standing alongside the girl again.

'OK, I'm taking it.' Kazu pointed the camera at the two. It didn't seem difficult to use, she just pressed the button that appeared in the screen.

Click

'What? Wait a bit, when are you going to take it?' said Kei.

Kazu had taken the picture while Kei was adjusting her hair and arranging her fringe. She handed the camera back to the girl.

'You already took it? When did you do that?' The girl and Kazu were both very businesslike. Kei alone was full of questions and confused.

'Thank you very much,' said the girl and immediately drank the remainder of her coffee.

'What . . . ? Just a minute,' Kei said. But the girl vaporized into steam. As the steam rose towards the ceiling, the woman in the dress appeared from underneath it. It looked like a transformation trick worthy of a ninja.

As all three were used to such things happening, no one was particularly surprised. If another customer had seen it they would have been shocked. If a customer ever did see such a thing they would be told it was a parlour trick – though if the cafe staff were asked how they performed this trick, they would be unable to provide an answer.

The woman in the dress was reading her novel casually as if nothing had happened. However, when she noticed the tray, she pushed it away with her right hand, which clearly meant: *Take that away!*

When Kei went to clean up the tray, Nagare took it from her, tilted his head to one side, and disappeared into the kitchen.

'I wonder who that was,' Kei muttered. She retrieved the plastic convenience-store bag and straw hat from Kazu and retreated to the back room.

Kazu kept staring at *that* chair where the woman in the

dress was sitting. It was clear by the look on her face that something was bothering her.

This was the first time a customer had come from the future to meet Nagare, Kei, or Kazu. There had never seemed to be a good reason why anyone would want to go back in time to see one of the cafe staff members who were always in the cafe.

Yet a girl had just come from the future to meet Kei.

Kazu didn't interrogate or press anyone on why they had visited from the future. Even if, say, a murderer travelled back in time, she would have a good reason to leave it alone: the rule was that the present doesn't change no matter how much one tries to rearrange things in the past. This rule could never be broken. A series of random events would always somehow unfold to prevent the present from changing. If, for example, a gunman came from the future and fatally shot a customer – as long as the customer was living in the future, he could not die, even if he had been shot in the heart.

That was the rule.

Kazu or whoever was there would call the ambulance and the police. The ambulance would leave for the cafe. This ambulance would not get caught in traffic. The ambulance would travel from the emergency centre to the cafe and carry the patient from the cafe to the hospital using the shortest distance and in the fastest time. On looking at the patient, the hospital staff might say, '*We probably can't save him.*' Even if that happened, then a world-leading surgeon would happen to be visiting the hospital and would operate on the patient. Even if the victim's blood was a rare type that only one in several ten thousand possessed, there would be a stock of such blood at the hospital. The surgery staff would be excellent and the operation would be successful. The surgeon might say later that if the ambulance had been one minute later or if the bullet had been located one millimetre to the left, the patient would not have survived. All the staff would say that it was a miracle the patient survived. But it wouldn't be a miracle. It would be because of the rule which dictated that the man who was shot in the past must survive.

Because of this, Kazu didn't mind who came from the future, for whatever reason. Everything a visitor from the future might try would be futile.

'Could you do this for me, please,' Nagare called from the kitchen.

Kazu turned and looked to see Nagare standing at the kitchen door holding the tray containing the coffee brewed for the woman in the dress. She took the tray and started carrying it to the table where the woman was sitting.

For a while she stared at the woman, while thoughts went around in her head. *What did that girl come back for, I wonder? If it was to take a picture of Kei, why did she go to the effort of returning to the past?*

CLANG-DONG

'Hello, welcome,' Nagare shouted. Kazu collected her thoughts and served the coffee.

(*I feel like there is something important that I'm missing.*)

To dispel the feeling, she gave her head a little shake.

'Hello.' Kohtake had entered the cafe. She was on her way home from work.

She was wearing a lime-green polo shirt and a white skirt with black pumps on her feet. She had a canvas bag hanging from her shoulder.

'Hello, Kohtake,' Nagare said.

On hearing her name called, she spun round on her heel as if to walk out again.

'Ah, sorry. Mrs Fusagi,' he corrected himself. Kohtake smiled with approval and sat at the counter.

It was now three days since Kohtake had returned to the past and received the letter that Fusagi had written but never given to her. She now insisted upon 'Mrs Fusagi'.

She hung her bag on the back of her chair. 'Coffee, please,' she ordered.

'Certainly,' Nagare said, bowing his head and turning to the kitchen to brew the coffee.

She looked around the empty cafe, flexed her shoulders, and took a deep breath. She had planned to accompany Fusagi on his walk home if he had been at the cafe, so she was a little disappointed. Kazu, who had been watching the exchange between Nagare and Kohtake with a smile, had finished serving the woman in the dress.

'I'm just taking my break,' she said and disappeared into the back room. Kohtake said, 'OK,' and gave her a little wave.

It was early August and summer was really peaking. Kohtake, though, liked her coffee hot, even in summer. She liked the aroma of it when it was freshly brewed. She couldn't enjoy iced coffee in the same way. Coffee was far more pleasurable when it was hot.

When Nagare made coffee, he usually brewed it using the siphon method, by pouring boiling water into a flask, then heating it to allow the evaporated steam to rise through a funnel and extract the coffee from the ground beans held inside the funnel. However, when he made coffee for Kohtake and some other regular customers, he brewed the coffee hand-drip style. When making hand-drip coffee, he put a paper filter in a dripper, added the ground beans, and poured boiling water over them. He thought the hand-drip style of making coffee allowed for greater flexibility as you could change the bitterness and sourness of the coffee by changing the temperature of the water, and the way you poured it. As the cafe did not play background music, it was possible to hear the soft sound of the coffee dripping, drop by drop, into the server. When Kohtake heard this dripping sound, she would smile in satisfaction.

Kei tended to use an automatic coffee maker. This machine was equipped with a single button that allowed different tastes to be accommodated. As Kei was not a master in the art of making coffee, she preferred to rely on a machine. Some of the regular customers who came to enjoy a cup of coffee did not therefore order when Nagare was not around. After all, the coffee was always the same price, whether it was brewed by Nagare or Kei. Kazu normally made coffee using the siphon method. The reason for this choice was not because of taste. She simply enjoyed watching the hot water rise up through the funnel. Besides, Kazu found the hand-drip coffee too tedious to make.

Kohtake was served with a coffee specially brewed by Nagare. With the coffee in front of her, she closed her eyes, and inhaled deeply. It was her moment of happiness. As per his insistence, the coffee had been made from mocha beans with their distinct aroma, which coffee drinkers either love or hate. Those who enjoy the aroma, like Kohtake, can't get enough of it. In fact, you could say that the coffee picked the customers. Just as with his butter, Nagare enjoyed watching customers take pleasure in the aroma. As he watched, his eyes narrowed even further.

'By the way,' said Kohtake while enjoying her coffee, as if she'd suddenly remembered, 'I noticed that Hirai's bar has been closed both yesterday and today. Do you know anything about that?'

The snack bar, a sort of mini-hostess bar, that Hirai ran was just metres from the cafe.

It was just a small bar comprising a counter with six seats, but it was always busy. It opened at different times each evening, depending on Hirai's mood, but it was open seven nights a week, all year round. Since she opened its doors, the bar had opened every night without fail. Patrons often waited outside for it to open. Some nights, as many as ten customers squeezed into the place. Only the first six customers sat on chairs; the rest would drink standing up.

The patrons weren't only men, either. Hirai was popular among women too. Her blunt way of speaking sometimes dented the pride of patrons, but they knew there was no malice intended, and there were never hard feelings. Patrons always felt comfortable around her; she had a natural gift for being able to say anything and get away with it. She dressed in a flashy way and couldn't care less what anyone thought about it. But she believed in good manners and etiquette. She would listen to anything anyone had to say. Though if she thought a patron was wrong, even if they were of high social status, she would have no qualms about setting them straight. Some patrons were generous with their money, but she never accepted any money except in payment for drinks. Some patrons would try to earn her favour by offering her expensive gifts, but she never accepted them, not once. There were even men who would offer her a house or an apartment, a Mercedes or a Ferrari, or diamonds or the like, but she would just say, 'I'm not interested.' Even Kohtake sometimes visited her bar. It was a place where you could be guaranteed to have a fun time drinking.

Kohtake had noticed that her bar, usually so full of customers, had been closed for two nights in a row, and none of the patrons knew why. She was a little concerned.

As soon as she broached the subject of Hirai, Nagare's face turned serious.

'What happened?' she asked, a little startled.

'Her sister. There was a road accident,' he said softly.

'Oh no!'

'So she went home.'

'Oh how terrible!' She sank her gaze into the pitch-black coffee. She knew Hirai's younger sister Kumi from when she would visit and try to get Hirai – who had broken ties with the family – to come home. For the last one or two years, Hirai had found her frequent visits such a nuisance that more often than not she avoided meeting her. Regardless, Kumi would make the visit to Tokyo almost every month. Three days ago,

Kumi had visited the cafe to meet Hirai. The accident occurred on her way home.

The small car that she was driving collided head on with an oncoming truck whose driver must have dozed off. She was taken to hospital in an ambulance but did not survive the journey.

'What horrible news.' Kohtake left her coffee alone.

The faint steam that had been rising from it had disappeared. Nagare stood with arms folded, silently looking at his feet.

He had received an email on his phone from Hirai. She probably would have contacted Kei, but Kei didn't own a phone. In the email, Hirai gave some details about the accident and mentioned that the bar would be closed for a while. The email had been written in a matter-of-fact tone, as if it had happened to someone else. Kei had used his phone to reply and had asked how Hirai was doing, but she got no response. The inn on the outskirts of Sendai was called Takakura, meaning 'The Treasury'.

Sendai is a popular tourist destination, particularly famous for its gorgeous Tanabata Festival. The festival is best known for its *sasakazari*: a towering piece of bamboo about ten metres long, to which five giant paper balls with colourful paper streamers are attached. Other decorations from the festival – colourful paper strips, paper kimonos, and origami paper cranes – are sought after by tourists who use them for business blessings and lucky charms. The festival always takes place from 6 to 8 August, which meant that in a few days, the decoration preparation in the downtown area around Sendai Station was due to begin. Given the two million tourists who

were attracted to the three-day festival, Tanabata was the busi-
est period for Takakura, located as it was about ten minutes by
taxi from Sendai Station.

CLANG-DONG

'Hello! Welcome,' Nagare called out cheerfully, lifting the cafe
out of its sombre mood.

On hearing the bell, Kohtake took the opportunity to get
more comfortable. She reached for the coffee.

'Hello. Welcome,' said Kei, coming out from the back room
in an apron after hearing the bell. But there was still no one.

It was taking longer than normal for someone to appear in
the cafe but just as Nagare tilted his head questioningly to one
side, a familiar voice rang out.

'Nagare! Kei! Someone! I need salt! Bring me salt!'

'Hirai, is that you?'

No one had expected her to have come back so early, even
if her sister's funeral had now taken place. Kei looked at
Nagare, her eyes wide in astonishment. Nagare stood there a
moment in a daze. Given that he'd just delivered the terrible
news about Kumi to Kohtake, to hear Hirai's usual brisk tone
must have been a little disorientating.

Hirai may have wanted the salt for spiritual purification,
but it sounded more like yelling coming from a kitchen where
someone was frantically making dinner.

'Come on!' This time, her shout had a low, sultry edge to it.

'OK! Just a sec.'

Nagare finally got moving. He grabbed a small bottle of
cooking salt from the kitchen and shuffled hastily to the

entrance. Kohtake pictured Hirai standing beyond the cafe's entrance, dressed in her normal flashy attire. To her, Hirai's behaviour wasn't quite what one might expect. *How could it be that her sister had just died?* She and Kei exchanged glances – Kei seemed to be thinking the same thing.

'I'm so exhausted,' Hirai said, coming in dragging her feet.

Her walk was the same as normal, but she was dressed rather differently. Rather than wearing her usual loud clothes in red and pink, she was in mourning dress. Rather than a head full of curlers, her hair was done up in a tight bun. Anyone would agree that she looked like a different person. Dressed in her mourning black, she dropped herself down at the middle table seat and raised her right arm.

'Sorry to be a bother, but could I have a glass of water, please?' she asked Kei.

'Of course,' Kei said.

With a somewhat exaggerated sense of urgency, she scuttled off to the kitchen to find some water.

'Phew,' Hirai exclaimed.

She stretched out her arms and legs like she was doing a star jump. Her black handbag swung from her right arm. Nagare, still holding the bottle of salt, and Kohtake, seated at the counter, stared at her like she was behaving oddly. Kei came back with a glass of water.

'Thank you.' Hirai put her handbag on the table, took the glass in her hand, and to Kei's amazement, drank it down in one gulp. She let out an exhausted sigh.

'Another one, please,' she said, presenting Kei with the glass. Kei took the glass and disappeared into the kitchen. Wiping perspiration from her brow, Hirai let out another sigh. Nagare stood there watching her.

'Hirai?' he said.

'What?'

'How do I put it?'

'Put what?'

'How do I say it? That . . .'

'What?'

'I'm sorry for your loss . . .'

Hirai's strange behaviour – so unlike someone in mourning – had made Nagare struggle to remember an appropriate thing to say. Kohtake was also lost for words and bowed her head.

'You mean Kumi?'

'Yes. Of course . . .'

'Well it was certainly unexpected. Unlucky, I guess you'd say,' Hirai said, shrugging her shoulders.

Kei returned with another glass of water. Worried about Hirai's demeanour, Kei handed her the glass and also bowed her head, revealing her discomfort.

'I'm sorry. Thanks.' Hirai downed the new glass of water as well. 'They said she got hit in the wrong place . . . so she was unlucky,' she said.

It sounded like she was talking about something that had happened to a stranger. The crease deepened between Kohtake's brows as she leant forward.

'Was it today?'

'What today?'

'The funeral, of course,' Kohtake replied, betraying her uneasiness with Hirai's attitude.

'Yeah. Look,' Hirai said as she stood up and spun round to show her funeral attire. 'It kind of suits me, don't you think? Do you think it makes me look a bit subdued?' Hirai made some model-like poses, adopting a proud face.

Her sister was dead. Unless the people in the cafe were mistaken about that, her irreverence seemed over the top.

As she became increasingly irritated at Hirai's blasé attitude, Kohtake strengthened her words. 'Why on earth did you come home so early . . . ?' she asked, her face showing signs of disgust as if she was biting her tongue, trying not to say, *A little disrespectful to your dead sister, don't you think?*

Hirai dropped her exaggerated pose and sat down again lazily.

She held up her hands.

'Oh, it's not like that. I've got the bar to think about too . . .' she answered, clearly knowing what Kohtake wanted to say.

'But still . . .'

'Please. Let it go.'

She reached over to her black handbag and took a cigarette from inside.

'So, are you OK?' Nagare asked, toying with the salt bottle in his hands.

'With what?' Hirai was reluctant to open up. With a cigarette in her mouth, she was peering into her black handbag again. She was rummaging around for her lighter, which she seemed to be having a job finding.

Nagare pulled a lighter from his pocket and presented it to her. 'But your parents must be very upset over the death of your sister. Shouldn't you have stayed to be with them for a while?'

Hirai took the lighter from Nagare and lit her cigarette. 'Well, sure . . . Normally that would be the case.'

Her cigarette glowed and burnt to a column of ash. She tapped the ash in the ashtray. The cigarette smoke rose and disappeared. Hirai watched the smoke rise.

'But there was nowhere for me to be,' she said, expression-less.

For a moment, what she had said did not sink in. Both Nagare and Kohtake looked at her uncomprehendingly.

Hirai saw how the two were looking at her. 'I didn't have a place where I could be,' she added, and took another drag of her cigarette.

'What do you mean?' Kei asked with a look of concern.

In answer to Kei's question, Hirai replied as if talking about any ordinary thing. 'The accident happened on her way home from seeing me, right? So naturally my parents blame me for her death.'

'How could they think that?' Kei asked with her mouth agape.

Hirai blew a plume of smoke into the air. 'Well they do . . . And in a way it's true,' she muttered dismissively. 'She kept coming down to Tokyo, time and time again . . . And each time, I would turn her away.'

The last time, Kei had helped Hirai avoid Kumi by hiding. She now looked down with a look of regret. Hirai continued talking, taking no notice of Kei.

'Both my parents refused to talk to me.' Hirai's smile faded from her face. 'Not one word.'

Hirai had heard of Kumi's death from the head waitress who had worked at her parents' inn for many years. It had been years since Hirai had answered a call coming from the inn. But two days ago, early in the morning, the inn's number flashed up on her phone. When she saw who it was, her heart skipped a beat and she answered it. The only thing she could say in response to the teary head waitress who was calling was, '*I see*,' and she hung up. Then she picked up her handbag and headed to her family home by taxi.

The taxi driver claimed to be a former entertainer. On their journey, he gave her an unsolicited sample of his comedic act. His stories were unexpectedly funny and she rolled around in the confines of the back seat roaring with laughter. She laughed long and hard, with tears streaming down her face. Finally the taxi pulled up in front of the inn, Takakura, Hirai's family home.

It was five hours from the city and the taxi fare was over 150,000 yen, but as she was paying in cash the driver said a nice round number was fine and drove off in high spirits.

When she got out of the taxi, she realized she was still wearing slippers. She also had curlers in her hair. Wearing only her camisole, she felt the hot morning sun hit her with its full force. When large beads of sweat began dripping down her body, she wished she had a handkerchief. She began to walk up the gravel path to her family home at the rear of the inn. Where her family lived was designed in Japanese-style and had not been altered in any way since it was built at the same time as the inn.

She passed the large-roofed gate and came to the front entrance. It had been thirteen years since she was last there, but nothing had changed. To her, it seemed a place where time stood still. She tried opening the sliding door. It was unlocked.

The door rattled open and she stepped into the concrete inside. It was cold. The chill of the air was enough to send a shiver down her spine. She walked from the entrance down the hall-way to the living room. The room was completely dark with no sign of life. This was quite normal. Rooms in old Japanese houses tended to be dark, but she found the darkness oppres-sive. The hallway was completely quiet except for the creaking of her footsteps. The family altar was in a room at the end of the hallway.

When she looked into the altar room, it was open to the veranda. There, she saw her father Yasuo's small rounded back. He was sitting on the edge, looking out at the lush green garden.

Kumi was lying there silently. She was dressed in a white robe, and had hanging over her the pink kimono worn by the head woman of the inn. Yasuo must have just moved from her side, as his hand was still gripping the white cloth that would normally cover the face of the dead. Her mother Michiko was not there.

Hirai sat down and peered at Kumi's face. So peaceful was it that it looked like she was merely sleeping. As Hirai gently touched her face, she whispered, *Thank God*. If her face had been badly cut in the accident, her body would have been laid in the coffin and wrapped up like a mummy. This is what was running through her mind as she looked at Kumi's pretty face. The thought had been troubling her, having heard that Kumi collided head on with a truck. Her father, Yasuo, kept gazing out at the courtyard garden.

'Father . . .' Hirai called out in a stilted voice to Yasuo's back.

It was to be her first conversation with her father since she left home thirteen years ago.

But Yasuo remained seated with his back to her, his only response being a sniffle. Hirai looked at Kumi's face a while longer, then slowly rose and quietly left the room.

She went into Sendai town, where preparations for the Tanabata Festival were under way. With curlers still in her hair, she trudged around until dusk, still in her slippers and camisole. She bought something to wear to the funeral and found a hotel.

At the funeral the next day, she saw her mother Michiko putting on a brave face alongside her father, who had broken down in tears. Rather than sitting in the row of seats for the family, she sat with the rest of the mourners. Just once she made eye contact with her mother, but no words passed between them. The funeral went smoothly. Hirai offered incense, but left without speaking to anyone.

The column of ash lengthened on Hirai's cigarette and fell silently. She watched it fall. 'Yes, and that's that,' she said, stubbing out the cigarette.

Nagare's head was bowed. Kohtake sat motionless with her cup in her hand.

Kei looked directly at Hirai with concern.

Hirai looked at these three faces and sighed. 'I'm no good with all this serious stuff,' she let out in exasperation.

'Hirai . . .' Kei began, but Hirai waved her hand to stop her.

'So lose the sad faces, and stop asking if I'm all right,' she pleaded.

She could see that there was something that Kei wanted to say. So she kept talking.

'I might not look like it, but I am really upset. But, come on, guys, I need to overcome this by putting my best foot forward, don't I?'

She spoke as if she was trying to reassure a tearful child. She was that kind of person – inscrutable to the end. If Kei was in her shoes, she would have been crying for days. If it were Kohtake, she would have observed the mourning period, lamented the deceased, and behaved with propriety. But Hirai was neither Kei nor Kohtake.

'I'll mourn how I mourn. Everyone's different,' Hirai said, and with that she stood up and picked up her handbag.

'So that's how things are,' she said, and began to walk to the door.

'So, why visit the cafe now?' Nagare muttered, as if to himself.

Hirai froze like a stop-motion frame.

'Why come here rather than going directly back to yours?' he asked bluntly, keeping his back to her. Hirai stood there silently for a while.

'Busted.' She sighed. She turned round and walked back to where she had been sitting.

Nagare didn't look at her. He just carried on staring at the bottle of salt in his hands.

She returned to her seat and sat down in the chair.

'Hirai,' Kei said as she approached holding a letter. 'I still have it.'

'You didn't throw it out?' She recognized it instantly. She was pretty sure it was the one Kumi had written and left at the cafe three days ago. She had asked Kei to throw it out without having read any of it.

Her hand trembled as she took it: the last letter that Kumi had ever written.

'I never imagined I would hand it to you under such circumstances,' Kei said with her head bowed apologetically.

'No of course not . . . Thank you,' Hirai replied.

She pulled out a letter folded in half from the unsealed envelope.

The contents were just as she had thought; it was always the same. But though the letter was filled with the same old irritating things, a single teardrop fell from her eyes.

'I didn't even meet her and now this happened,' she said, sniffing. 'Only she never gave up on me. She came to Tokyo to see me again and again.'

The first time Kumi came to visit Hirai in Tokyo, Hirai was twenty-four and Kumi was eighteen. But back then, Kumi was the *cuddly little sister* who contacted her every now and then behind her parents' back. Still only in senior high school, she was already helping at the inn when she wasn't at school. When Hirai left home, her parents' expectations were immediately transferred to Kumi. Before she had even come of age, she had become the face of the old inn, the future owner. Kumi's efforts to persuade Hirai to return to the family began then. Despite always being busy with her responsibilities, Kumi found the time to visit Tokyo once every couple of months. At first, while Hirai still saw Kumi as her cuddly younger sister, she would meet her and listen to what she had to say. But there came a point where Kumi's requests began to feel like an annoying imposition. For the last year, the last two years for that matter, Hirai had completely avoided her.

The final time, she had hidden from her in this very cafe, and tried to throw away what Kumi had written to her. She put the letter that Kei had rescued back in the envelope.

'I know the rule. The present doesn't change no matter how hard you try. I fully understand that. Take me back to that day.'

'. . .'

'I'm begging you!' Hirai's face was now far more serious than it ever had been. She bowed her head deeply.

Nagare's narrow eyes narrowed further as he looked down at Hirai bowing deeply. Naturally, Nagare knew the day that Hirai was referring to: three days ago when Kumi had visited the cafe. She was asking to go back and meet her. Kei and Kohtake waited with bated breath for Nagare's reply. The room became eerily silent. Only the woman in the dress continued to behave as if nothing was wrong, continuing to read her novel.

Plonk.

The sound of Nagare putting the bottle of salt on the counter echoed throughout the cafe.

Then, without a word, he walked away and disappeared into the back room.

Hirai lifted her head, and took a large, deep breath.

From the back room, Nagare's voice could be faintly heard calling for Kazu.

'But, Hirai—'

'Yeah, I know.'

Hirai interrupted Kohtake so she didn't have to hear what she was going to say. She walked up to the woman in the dress.

'Um, so like I was just saying to the others. Could I sit there, please?'

'Hi— Hirai!' Kei said frantically.

'Can you do this for me? Please!' Ignoring Kei, Hirai put her hands together as if she were praying to a god. She looked faintly ridiculous as she did so, but still she seemed genuinely serious.

But the woman in the dress did not even flinch. This made Hirai irate. 'Hey! Can you hear me? Don't just ignore me. Can't you give me the seat?' she said while putting her hand on the woman's shoulder.

'No! Hirai, stop! You mustn't.'

'Please!' She wasn't listening to Kei. She tried to pull the woman's arm by force, to take the seat from her.

'Hirai, stop it!' Kei yelled.

But at that moment, the woman in the dress's eyes opened wide, and she glared at Hirai. Instantly, she was overwhelmed by the sensation that she was becoming heavier, many times over. It felt as if the earth's gravity had begun multiplying. The cafe's lighting suddenly seemed reduced to candlelight, flickering in the wind, and an eerie ghostly wailing began reverberating throughout the cafe, with no sign of where it was coming from. Unable to move a muscle, she fell to her knees.

'What the . . . what is this?'

'Well, you could have listened!' Kei sighed dramatically, with an air of I-told-you-so.

Hirai was familiar with the rules, but she didn't know anything about the curse. What she knew had been put together from explanations given to customers who had come wanting to go back to the past, and they had normally given up on the idea after hearing the overly complicated rules.

'She's a demon . . . a hag!' she shouted.

'No, she's just a ghost,' Kei interjected coolly. From the floor, Hirai was hurling insults at the woman in the dress, but such abuse was useless.

'Oh . . .!' Kazu exclaimed when she appeared from the back room. One look told her what had happened. She darted back into the kitchen and came out carrying a carafe filled with coffee. She walked up to the woman in the dress.

'Would you care for some more coffee?' Kazu asked.

'Yes, please,' the woman in the dress replied, and Hirai was released. Strangely, Kazu was the only one who could lift the curse; when Kei or Nagare had tried to it hadn't worked. Now free, Hirai returned to normal. She started panting heavily. Looking very worn out by the ordeal, she turned to Kazu.

'Kazu love, please say something to her. Get her to move!' she cried.

'OK, I understand what you're going through, Hirai.'

'So can you do something?'

Kazu looked down at the carafe she was holding in her hands. She thought for a few moments.

'I can't say whether this will work or not . . .'

Hirai was desperate enough to try anything.

'Whatever! Please do this for me!' she pleaded, holding her hands in prayer.

'OK, let's try it.' Kazu walked up to the woman in the dress. With Kei's help, Hirai returned to standing and watched to see what was about to happen.

'Would you care for some more coffee?' Kazu asked again despite the cup being still full to the brim.

Hirai and Kohtake both tilted their heads sideways, unable to work out what Kazu was doing.

But the woman in the dress responded to the offer of a refill.

'Yes, please,' she replied, and drank the entire cup of coffee that had been poured for her just moments before. Kazu then filled the emptied cup with coffee. The woman in the dress then proceeded to read her novel, as if nothing out of the ordinary had happened.

Then, straight afterwards . . .

'Would you care for some more coffee?' Kazu asked again.

The woman in the dress still had not touched the coffee since the last refill: the cup remained completely full.

And yet the woman in the dress again replied, 'Yes, please,' and proceeded to down the entire coffee.

'Well, who would have thought . . .' Kohtake said, her expression slowly changing as she realized what Kazu was doing.

Kazu continued with her outlandish plan. After filling the cup with coffee she would offer again: 'Would you care for some more coffee?' She went on doing this, and every time it was offered, the woman in the dress would reply, 'Yes, please,' and drink it down. But after a while, the woman began to look uncomfortable.

Rather than drinking the coffee down in one go, she began to take several sips to finish it. Using this method, Kazu managed to get the woman in the dress to drink seven cups of coffee.

'She looks so uncomfortable. Why doesn't she just refuse?' Kohtake commented, sympathizing with the woman in the dress.

'She can't refuse,' Kei whispered in Kohtake's ear.

'Why not?'

'Because apparently that's the rule.'

'Goodness . . .' Kohtake said in surprise to the fact that it wasn't only those travelling back in time who had to follow annoying rules. She watched on, eager to see what would happen next. Kazu poured an eighth coffee, filling the cup almost to the point of overflowing. The woman in the dress winced. But Kazu was relentless.

'Would you care for some more coffee?'

When Kazu offered the ninth cup of coffee, the woman in the dress suddenly stood up from her seat.

'She stood up!' Kohtake exclaimed in excitement.

'Toilet,' the woman in the dress mumbled, glaring directly at Kazu, and headed off to the toilet.

It had taken some coercion, but *that* seat had been vacated.

'Thank you,' Hirai said as she staggered over to the seat where the woman in the dress had been sitting. Hirai's nervousness seemed to affect everyone in the cafe. She drew in a large, deep breath, slowly exhaled, and slid in between the table and the chair. She sat down and gently closed her eyes.

Kumi Hirai had always been, since she was a young girl, a little sister who followed her big sister around, calling out 'Big Sis' this and 'Big Sis' that.

The old inn was always very busy, no matter the season. Her father was the proprietor and her mother the proprietress.

Her mother Michiko went back to work soon after she was born. Often the task of watching over her, still a young baby, fell to six-year-old Hirai. When she started elementary school, Hirai would give her a piggyback to school. It was a country school, and the teachers were understanding. If she started crying in class, Hirai was able to take her out of class to comfort her. In school Hirai was a reliable big sister, diligent in looking after her little sister.

Hirai's parents had great hopes for Hirai, who was naturally sociable and likeable. They thought she would become an excellent manager of the inn. But her parents had underestimated the intricacies of her character. Specifically, she was free-spirited. She wanted to do things without having to worry what others thought. It was what made her comfortable enough to give Kumi a piggyback to school. She had no inhibitions. She wanted to do things her own way. Her behaviour meant that her parents didn't worry about her, but it was precisely this free-spiritedness that ultimately led to her refusal of her parents' wish that she would someday take over the inn.

She didn't hate her parents, nor did she hate the inn. She simply lived for her freedom. At eighteen, she left home, when Kumi was twelve. Her parents' anger at her leaving home was just as intense as the expectation they had held that she would be their successor, and they cut her off. While the shock of her leaving weighed heavy on her parents, Kumi also took it badly.

But Kumi must have sensed that she was going to leave. When she left, Kumi did not cry or appear heartbroken; she just muttered, 'She's so selfish,' when she saw the letter that Hirai had left for her.

*

Kazu was standing beside Hirai and carrying a white coffee cup and silver kettle on a silver tray. Her face had an elegant, calm expression.

'You know the rules?'

'I know the rules . . .'

Kumi had visited the cafe, and while it wouldn't be possible to change the fact that she died in the accident, Hirai was now sitting in the right seat, and however short the time she would have in the past, if she could see Kumi one last time, it would be worth it.

Hirai gave a deep nod and prepared herself.

But regardless of her preparedness, Kazu continued to speak.

'People who go back to the past to meet a person now deceased can get caught up in the emotion, so even though they know there is a time limit, they become unable to say goodbye. So I want you to have this . . .' Kazu placed a small stick about ten centimetres long into Hirai's cup of coffee – the kind you might use to stir a cocktail. It looked a bit like a spoon.

'What's this?'

'This sounds an alarm just before the coffee gets cold. So if the alarm sounds—'

'OK. I know. I understand, OK?'

The vagueness of the deadline 'just before the coffee gets cold' worried Hirai. Even if *she* thought the coffee was cold, there still might be time remaining. Or she might think the coffee still had enough heat in it and make the mistake of staying too long and never making it back. An alarm made things much simpler and calmed her anxiety.

All she wanted to do was apologize. Kumi had made the effort to come to visit her time and time again but Hirai saw it only as a nuisance.

Apart from the matter of how she had treated Kumi so unkindly, there was also the matter of Kumi being made the successor to Takakura.

When Hirai left home and was cut off from the family, Kumi automatically became the successor. She was too obliging to betray the expectations of their parents, as Hirai had done.

But what if this had shattered a dream that she held?

If she once had a dream, ruined by Hirai's selfish decision to run away, it would explain why she had so often visited Hirai to beg her to return home – she would want Hirai to come back so that she could have the freedom to pursue her own ambitions.

If Hirai had found her freedom at Kumi's expense, then it would only be natural for her to feel resentful. Now there was no way of ending Hirai's regret.

This was all the more reason for her to apologize. If she could not change the present, then at least she could say, '*Sorry, please forgive your selfish big sis.*'

Hirai looked into Kazu's eyes and gave a firm, definite nod.

Kazu put the coffee in front of Hirai. She picked up the silver kettle from the tray with her right hand and looked at Hirai from underneath her lowered brow. This was the ceremony. The ceremony did not change, no matter who was sitting in *that* seat. Kazu's expressions were part of it.

'Just remember . . .' Kazu paused and then whispered, 'Drink the coffee before it goes cold.'

She began to slowly pour the coffee, which flowed sound-lessly from the silver kettle's narrow spout, like a single black thread. Hirai watched the surface of the liquid as it rose. The longer the coffee took to fill the cup, the more impatient she became. She wanted to go back and meet her little sister with-out delay. She wanted to see her, to apologize. But the coffee would start cooling the moment the cup was filled – she had precious little time.

Shimmering steam rose from the filled cup. Looking at it, Hirai began to experience an overwhelming dizziness. Her body became one with the steam that engulfed her, and she felt like she was beginning to rise. Although it was the first time experiencing this, she didn't find it at all frightening. Feel-ing her impatience subside, she gently closed her eyes.

Hirai first visited the cafe seven years before. She was twenty-four and had been running her bar for about three months. One Sunday at the end of autumn she was strolling around the neighbourhood and casually popped into the cafe to check it out. The only customers were a woman in a white dress and herself. It was the time of the year when people started wearing scarves, but the woman in the dress was in short sleeves. Think-ing that she must be a little chilly, even if she was inside, Hirai sat down at the counter.

She looked around the room, but there were no staff mem-bers in sight. When the bell had rung as she entered the cafe, she hadn't heard anyone call out 'Hello, welcome!' as she might have expected. She got the impression that this cafe was not big on customer service, but this didn't put her off. The kind of place that didn't follow conventions appealed to her.

She decided to wait to see if anyone who worked there would make an appearance. Perhaps sometimes the bell went unnoticed? She was suddenly curious as to whether this often happened. Also, the woman in the dress had not even noticed her; she just kept on reading her book. Hirai got the feeling that she had mistakenly stumbled into the cafe on a day when it was closed. After about five minutes, the bell rang and in came a girl who looked like she might be in junior high school. She casually said, 'Hello, welcome,' without any sense of urgency and walked off into the back room. Hirai was over-joyed by this: she had found a cafe that didn't pander to cus-tomers. That meant freedom. There was no way of anticipating just when one would get served. She liked this kind of cafe – it was a refreshing change from the places that treated you in the same old predictable way. She lit a cigarette and waited leisurely.

After a short while, a woman appeared from the back room. By this time, Hirai was smoking her second cigarette. The woman was wearing a beige knit cardigan and a long white skirt with a wine-red apron over it. She had big round eyes.

The schoolgirl must have told her that they had a customer, but she entered the room in a laid-back, casual manner.

The woman with the big round eyes showed no sense of hurry. She poured some water into a glass and set it in front of Hirai. 'Hello, welcome.' She smiled as if everything was normal. A customer who expected to be treated in a special manner might have expected an apology for the slow service at least. But Hirai didn't want or expect such service. The woman didn't show any sign that she had behaved wrongly but instead smiled warmly. Hirai had never met another uninhibited woman who did things at her own pace, as she always did herself. She took an instant liking to her. *Treat them mean, keep them keen*, that was Hirai's motto.

From then on, Hirai started visiting Funiculi Funicula every day. During that winter she discovered that the cafe could *return you to the past*. She thought it was odd that the woman in the dress was always in short sleeves. When she asked, 'She must be cold, don't you think?' Kei explained about the woman in the dress, and how you could return to the past if you sat in that seat.

Hirai replied, 'You don't say?' though it sounded unbelievable to her. But as she didn't think Kei would tell a lie like that, she let it go for the time being. It was about six months later that the urban legend surrounding the cafe spread and its popularity grew.

But even once Hirai knew about travelling to the past, she never once considered doing so herself. She lived life in the fast lane and had no regrets. And what was the point anyway, she thought, if the rules meant that you couldn't change the present, no matter how hard you tried?

That was, until Kumi died in a traffic accident.

Amidst the shimmering, Hirai suddenly heard her name being called. When she heard this familiar voice, she opened her eyes with a start. Looking in the direction of the voice, she saw Kei standing there, wearing a wine-red apron. Her big round eyes showed she was surprised to see Hirai. Fusagi was in the cafe, sitting at the table closest to the entrance. It was exactly the scene that Hirai remembered. She had returned to that day – the day when Kumi was still alive.

Hirai felt her heartbeat quicken. She had to relax. The tension felt like cords stretched as far as they would go as she struggled to maintain her fragile composure. She pictured her eyes becoming red and swollen with tears and becoming choked up. That was not at all how she wanted to look when she met Kumi. She placed her hand on her heart, inhaled slowly and deeply to settle herself.

'Hello . . .' she greeted Kei.

Kei was caught by surprise at having someone she knew suddenly appear in that seat. Looking both startled and intrigued, she addressed Hirai as if it was the first time she had had such a visitor.

'What . . . You came from the future?'

'Yeah.'

'Really? What on earth for?'

The Kei of the past had no idea about what happened. It was a straight question, innocently asked.

'Oh, I've just come to see my sister.' Hirai wasn't in a position to lie. She tightened her grip on the letter she held in her lap.

'The one who is always coming to persuade you to come home?'

'That's the one.'

'Well, that makes a change! Aren't you normally trying to avoid her?'

'Well not today . . . Today, I'm going to see her.'

Hirai did her best to reply cheerfully. She had meant to laugh, but her eyes were not laughing. She was unable to produce a single twinkle. She didn't know where to direct her gaze, either. If Kei got a good look at her, she would see straight through her. Even now, she knew that Kei could sense that something was wrong.

'Did something happen?' Kei asked in a whisper.

She couldn't say anything for a while. Then in an unconvincing tone she said, 'Oh nothing. Nothing.'

Water flows from high places to low places. That is the nature of gravity. Emotions also seem to act according to gravity. When in the presence of someone with whom you have a bond, and to whom you have entrusted your feelings, it is hard to lie and get away with it. The truth just wants to come flowing out. This is especially the case when you are trying to hide your sadness or vulnerability. It is much easier to conceal sadness from a stranger, or from someone you don't trust. Hirai saw Kei as a confidante with whom she could share anything. The emotional gravity was strong. Kei was able to accept anything – forgive anything – that Hirai let flow out. A single kind word from Kei could cut the cords of tension that ran through her.

At that moment, it would have been enough for Kei to say just one more kind thing and the truth would have come pouring out. Kei was looking at her with concern. Hirai could tell, even without looking, and was therefore desperately avoiding looking at her.

Kei came out from behind the counter, bothered by Hirai's reluctance to look at her.

CLANG-DONG

Just then the bell rang.

'Hello, welcome!' said Kei, coming to a standstill as she automatically called out to the entrance.

But Hirai knew it was Kumi. The hands of the middle wall clock said it was three o'clock, and Hirai knew that the middle clock was the only one of the three that showed the correct time. This was the time that Kumi had visited the cafe three days earlier.

On that day, Hirai had been forced to hide behind the counter. The arrangement of the cafe – located in a basement with only one entrance – left her no choice. The only way in or out was via the stairs that led to the street. Hirai always turned up at the cafe after lunchtime. She would order coffee, chat with Kei, and then head off for work. That day, she had stood up from her seat, planning to open her bar early. She remembered looking at the middle wall clock to check the time: exactly three o'clock. A little early, but she thought she might try her hand at making some snacks for a change. She had finished paying for coffee and was just about to leave. She actually had her hand on the door when she heard Kumi's voice from the top of the stairs.

Kumi was coming down while talking to someone on the phone. In a panic, Hirai doubled back into the cafe and ran to hide behind the counter. *Clang-dong*, the bell rang. Hirai glimpsed Kumi entering the room as she ducked down. That was the story of her not meeting her sister three days earlier.

Now, Hirai was sitting in *that* seat, waiting for Kumi to come walking in. She realized she couldn't imagine what clothes Kumi would be wearing. She hadn't seen her face properly for years, in fact, she couldn't remember the last time she had. It made her realize just how consistently she had avoided her sister's visits. Now, her chest was full of regret. The pain intensified as she recalled the lowly tactics she had employed to avoid meeting her.

But right there in that moment, she could not allow herself to cry. She had never once cried in front of her sister. That meant Kumi would not consider it normal if she broke down in front of her now. She would want to know if something had happened. Put in that position, Hirai thought she would crumble. Despite knowing that the present would not change, she would nevertheless say, *'You have a car crash, take the train home!'* or *'Don't go home today!'* But that would be the worst thing that she could say. She would end up being the harbinger of death, upsetting Kumi beyond measure. She had to avoid that happening at all costs. Causing her further suffering was the last thing she wanted to do. She took a deep breath to try to calm her unwieldy emotions.

'Big Sis?'

Hearing that voice, Hirai's heart skipped a beat. It was Kumi's voice, a voice she'd thought she would never hear again. She slowly opened her eyes to see her sister at the entrance looking back at her.

'Hi there . . .' Hirai lifted her hand, waved and smiled as widely as she could. The strained look that she had been wearing was gone. But in her lap, clenched in her left hand, was the letter. Kumi stared at her.

Hirai could understand her confusion. Until now, every time Hirai had seen her, she made no effort to hide her awkwardness. She normally adopted a coldness to convey to her that she just wanted her to hurry up and leave. But this time was different. She was actually looking at Kumi and giving her a full-faced smile. Usually reluctant to even make eye contact, she was now looking at her and nothing else.

'Wow . . . This is strange. What's up with you today?'

'What do you mean?'

'I mean, in all these years, you've never been so easy to find.'

'You think?'

'I know!'

'Oh, Kumi, I'm sorry about that,' Hirai said, shrugging her shoulders.

Kumi slowly approached her, as if she was starting to feel more comfortable with her apparent change of heart.

'Um. Could I order, please? I'd like a coffee, some toast, and then curry rice and a mixed parfait?' she called out to Kei, who was standing behind the counter.

'I'll get right on it,' Kei said, glancing briefly over at Hirai.

Recognizing the Hirai she knew, she seemed much more at ease as she disappeared into the kitchen.

'Can I sit here?' Kumi asked Hirai hesitantly, as she pulled out the chair.

'Of course,' Hirai replied with a smile.

Elated, Kumi broke into a smile. Taking the chair opposite, she slowly sat down.

For a while neither talked. They just looked at each other. Kumi kept fidgeting and couldn't seem to relax. Hirai just kept looking at her, happy just to stare. Kumi returned her steady gaze.

'It's definitely pretty strange today,' she mumbled.

'How so?'

'It feels like something we haven't done for ages . . . just sitting here looking at each other . . .'

'We haven't?'

'Oh, come on. Last time I came, I was standing at your front door and you wouldn't let me in. The time before that you ran away with me chasing after you. Before that, you crossed the street to avoid me, and then before that . . .'

'Pretty awful, wasn't it?' Hirai agreed.

She knew that Kumi could keep on going on. It was obvious what was really happening – when she pretended not to be home when her apartment lights were on, when she acted like she was really drunk and said, 'Who are you?' pretending that she didn't recognize her. She never read Kumi's letters, she just threw them away. Even the very last letter. She was an awful big sis.

'Well that's how you are.'

'I'm sorry, Kumi. I'm really sorry,' Hirai said, poking her tongue out, trying to lift the mood.

Kumi couldn't let it go unremarked. 'So tell me the truth, what's happened?' she asked with a worried look.

'Huh? What do you mean?'

'Come on, you're acting all weird.'

'You think?'

'Has something happened?'

'No . . . nothing like that,' Hirai said, trying to sound natural.

The awkwardness and worry in Kumi's look made Hirai feel like it was her who was living her final hours, like someone in a sentimental television drama suddenly redeeming herself in the face of death. She felt her eyes redden at the cruel irony. She wasn't the one who was going to die. Overwhelmed by a wave of emotion, she could no longer maintain eye contact and lowered her gaze.

'Here we go . . .' Kei appeared with the coffee just in time.

Hirai quickly lifted her face again.

'Thank you,' Kumi said, politely nodding.

'Not at all.' Kei placed the coffee on the table, gave a little bow, and returned to behind the counter.

The flow of conversation had been interrupted. Hirai was lost for words. Ever since Kumi had appeared in the cafe, Hirai had wanted to hug her tightly and yell, *'Don't die!'* The effort alone of not saying this was keeping her busy.

As the pause in the conversation grew longer, Kumi began to get restless. She was fidgeting out of discomfort. Bending a letter pad she held on her lap, she kept glancing at the ticking wall clock. Hirai could see what she was thinking by how she was behaving.

Kumi was choosing her words carefully. Looking down, she was rehearsing in her head what she wanted to say. Of course the request in itself was simple – *Please come home*. But articulating this was a struggle.

It was so hard to say because every time she'd raised it over the last several years, Hirai had flatly refused, and the more she had repeatedly declined and refused, the colder she had become. Kumi had never given up, no matter how many times her sister refused, but she never got used to hearing *no*. Each time she heard it, it hurt her – and it made her sad.

When Hirai thought about how hard it must have been for Kumi to have been made to feel this way again and again, the tension in her chest felt like it had reached breaking point and snapped. For so long, Kumi had had to bear these feelings. At that moment, she was imagining that Hirai would once again refuse, and naturally, this left her at a loss. Each time, she battled tenaciously to find courage. But she never gave up, ever. She looked up and stared directly and boldly into Hirai's eyes. Hirai didn't look away; she looked directly back at Kumi, who took a short breath and was about to speak.

'OK, I don't mind coming home,' Hirai replied.

Technically it wasn't a reply because Kumi hadn't said anything yet. But Hirai had known all too well what she was going to ask and so responded to what she expected her to say: 'I want you to come home!'

Kumi's face betrayed her confusion, as if she didn't understand what Hirai had said. 'What?'

Hirai responded gently and clearly. 'OK . . . I don't mind going home to Takakura.'

Kumi's face still showed disbelief. 'Really?'

'But you know I wouldn't be much use, don't you?' Hirai said apologetically.

'That's OK. No problem! You can just learn the work as you go. Dad and Mum will be so pleased, I'm sure!'

'Really?'

'Of course they will!' Kumi replied and made a deep nod. Her face swiftly turned red and she burst into tears.

'What's up?'

This time it was Hirai's turn to be dismayed. She knew the reason for Kumi's tears: if Hirai returned to Takakura, she would reclaim her freedom. Her persistent efforts over so many years to persuade Hirai had paid off. It was no wonder that she was happy. But Hirai had never imagined it would lead to so much crying.

'This has always been my dream,' Kumi muttered, looking down, her tears spilling onto the table.

Hirai's heart beat wildly. So Kumi did have her own dreams. She had wanted to do something too. Hirai's selfishness had robbed her of that – a dream worth crying over.

She thought she should know exactly what she had got in the way of.

'What dream?' she asked Kumi.

With red teary eyes, Kumi looked up and took a deep breath. 'To run the inn together. With you,' she replied. Her face transformed into a big smile.

Never had Hirai seen Kumi show such an ecstatic, happy smile.

Hirai thought back to what she had said to Kei on this day in the past.

'*She resents me.*'

'*She didn't want it passed down to her.*'

'*I keep telling her I don't want to go home. But she keeps on asking time and time and time again. Saying that she was persistent would be an understatement.*'

'*I don't want to see it . . .*'

'*I see it written on her face. Because of what I did, she is now going to be owner of an inn she doesn't want to run. She wants me to come home so that she can be free.*'

'*I feel she is pressuring me.*'

'*Throw it away!*'

'*I can imagine what it says . . . It's really tough for me by myself. Please come home. It's OK if you learn the ropes once you come . . .*'

Hirai had said all those things. But she was wrong. Kumi didn't resent her. Nor was it true that she didn't want to inherit the inn. The reason that Kumi didn't give up trying to persuade Hirai to return was because *that* was her dream. It wasn't because she wanted her own freedom, and it wasn't because she was blaming her: it was her dream to run the inn together with Hirai. That dream had not changed, and nor had her little sister, who was there in front of her with tears of joy streaming down her face. Her little sister Kumi, who had loved her big sis with all her heart, had, time after time, come to persuade her to return to the family, never giving up. While her parents had disowned her, Kumi had hung on to the belief that Hirai would come home. How sweet her little sister still was. Always the little girl, always following her around. *'Big Sis! Big Sis!'* Hirai felt more love for Kumi than she ever had before.

But the little sister that she so loved was now gone.

Hirai's sense of regret grew. *Don't die on me! I don't want you to die!*

'Ku-Kumi.' Hirai called her name in a soft voice, as if it had just slipped out. Even if the effort was futile, she wanted to stop Kumi's death. But Kumi didn't seem to have heard Hirai.

'Wait a bit. Got to go to the toilet. I just need to fix my make-up,' Kumi said getting up from her seat and walking away.

'Kumi!' Hirai cried out.

Hearing her name suddenly screamed in that way stopped Kumi in her tracks. 'What?' she asked, looking startled.

Hirai didn't know what to say. Nothing she said would change the present.

'Er. Nothing. Sorry.'

Of course it wasn't nothing. *Don't go! Don't die! Sorry!*

Please forgive me! If you hadn't come to meet me, you wouldn't have died!

There were many things she wanted to say, and apologize for: selfishly leaving home, expecting Kumi to look after their parents, leaving it to her to take on the role of heir. Not only had she neglected to think how hard that was for her family, she'd never imagined what really led Kumi to take time from her busy schedule and come to see her. *I see now that you suffered by having me as your older sister. I'm sorry.* But none of these feelings could be formed into words. She had never understood . . . But what should she say? And what did she want to say?

Kumi was looking at her kindly. Even if nothing was forthcoming, she still waited for her to speak – she understood that she had something she wanted to say.

How kindly you look at me after I've been so horrible for so long. You held on to these kind feelings while you continued to wait for me for so long. Always wishing we could work together at the inn. Never giving up. But I . . .

After a long silence of being lost in her feelings Hirai managed to mutter just two words. 'Thank you.'

She didn't know whether that one phrase could contain all these feelings or whether it conveyed how she felt. But every part of her at that moment was invested in those two words.

Kumi looked perplexed for a moment, but then replied with a big grin. 'Yeah, you're definitely acting strange today.'

'Yeah, I guess,' Hirai said, squeezing out her last strength to produce her biggest and best smile. Visibly happy, Kumi shrugged and then twirled round and headed for the toilet.

Hirai watched her walk away. Tears welled up in her eyes. She felt she could no longer stem the flow. Yet she did not blink. She fixed her gaze on Kumi's back, watching her until she disappeared. As soon as Kumi was out of sight, she dropped her head and her tears fell from her face and landed like rain on the table. She felt the grief surge from the bottom of her heart. She wanted to scream and bawl, but she couldn't cry out.

If she did, Kumi would hear it. She desperately covered her mouth to stop herself from yelling her sister's name and with shoulders trembling she muted her voice and cried. From the kitchen, Kei called out to her, concerned by her strange behaviour.

'You OK, Hirai?'

Beep beep beep beep beep . . .

The sudden sound came from the coffee cup: the alarm warning that the coffee was about to get cold.

'Oh no! That alarm!'

Kei understood everything when she heard it – the alarm was only used when a person was visiting someone who had died.

Oh dear . . . Her sweet little sister . . .

With Kumi in the toilet, Kei looked over at Hirai. 'Surely no . . .' she muttered in dread.

Hirai saw how Kei was looking at her, and simply nodded sadly.

Kei looked distressed. 'Hirai,' she called.

'I know,' she said, grabbing the coffee cup. 'I've got to drink up, right?'

Kei didn't say anything. She couldn't say anything.

Hirai held the cup. She breathed in and exhaled with a moan, filled with all the painful grief seeping from her heart.

'I just want to see her face, one more time. But if I do, I won't be able to return.'

Hirai's shaking hands brought the cup to her lips. She had to drink up. Tears surged once again from her eyes. A rush of thoughts crossed her mind. *Why did this happen? Why did she have to die? Why didn't I say that I would go home earlier?*

The cup stopped a short distance from her lips and didn't move. After a moment, 'Ugh. I can't drink it . . .'

She put the cup down, totally drained of strength. She had no idea what she wanted to do or why she had gone back to the past. All she knew was that she loved her little sister, she was precious to her, and now she was gone.

If I drink this coffee now, I will never see my sister again. Even though I finally made her smile, it will never happen again. Yet she knew she would never be able to drink the coffee with Kumi's face in front of her.

'Hirai!'

'I can't drink it!'

Kei could see how distressed Hirai was. She bit her lip and looked grave.

'You just promised . . .' she said with a trembling voice. 'You just promised your sister, didn't you? That you would return to the inn.'

Kumi's happy elated smile was branded onto the back of her closed eyelids.

'You said that you would run it alongside her.'

Hirai imagined that Kumi was alive. They were working happily together at the inn.

The sound of that early morning phone call rang in her head. 'But she . . .'

The image of Kumi lying there as if she was sleeping flashed before her. Kumi was gone.

What was she to do once she returned to the present? Her heart seemed to have lost all desire to return. Kei was crying too, but Hirai had never heard such determination in her voice. 'That means you have to return. That makes it more important than ever.'

How so?

'How unhappy would your sister be if she knew that your promise was only made for today? She would be devastated, don't you think?'

Yes! Kei's right. Kumi told me it was her dream to work with me, and I promised her. That was the first time I had ever seen Kumi so happy. I can't act as if that smiling face never happened. I can't let her down again. I have to return to the present and to Takakura. Even if Kumi is dead, I promised her when she was alive. I have to make sure her happiness was for something.

Hirai grabbed the cup. But . . .

I want to see Kumi's face one more time. That was her last dilemma.

But waiting to see Kumi's face would mean not being able to return to the present. This was something that Hirai was all too aware of. Yet even though she knew that she had to just drink up the coffee, the distance between the cup and her mouth remained the same.

Clack.

She faintly heard the sound of the toilet door opening. At the moment she heard that sound, her instincts took over and she downed the coffee – she couldn't afford to hesitate.

All rational thinking had been put aside. She felt her entire body reacting intuitively. The moment she drank the coffee the dizziness returned and she felt like she was blending into the steam that now surrounded her entire body. She resigned herself to never seeing Kumi ever again. But just then she returned from the toilet.

Kumi!

Amidst the shimmering, part of Hirai's consciousness was still in the past.

'Huh? Big Sis?' Kumi had returned, but she seemed unable to see Hirai. She was looking at *that* seat, the one Hirai had been sitting in, with a puzzled look on her face.

Kumi!

Hirai's voice did not reach her.

The now-fading Kumi looked at Kei, who was standing with her back turned behind the counter.

'Excuse me, I don't suppose you know where my sister went, do you?' she asked.

Kei turned round and smiled at her. 'She had to go suddenly . . .'

On hearing this Kumi looked bereft. It must have been a disappointment. She finally met her sister and then she suddenly left. She had said she would return home, but the reunion was short and sweet. It was only natural that she felt anxious. She sighed and slumped in her chair. Kei saw how she reacted to this news.

'Don't worry! Your sister said she would keep her promise,'

she said, winking in the direction of where Hirai, reduced to steam, was watching.

Kei, you're a saviour! Thank you.

Hirai began crying, touched by Kei's support.

Kumi stood and was silent for a moment. 'Really?' she asked, as a broad smile spread over her face. 'OK, great! Well I'll be on my way home then.' She bowed politely then rose and walked out of the cafe with a spring in her step.

'*Kumi-i!*'

Hirai saw everything through shimmering steam. Kumi had smiled when she heard that Hirai would keep her promise.

Everything around Hirai wound from start to finish like a film on fast-forward. She continued to cry. She cried and cried and cried . . .

The woman in the dress had returned from the toilet and was standing next to her. Kazu, Nagare, Kohtake, and Kei were there too. Hirai had returned to the present – the present without Kumi.

The woman in the dress paid no attention to Hirai's teary eyes. 'Move!' she said disgruntledly.

'Ah. Right,' Hirai said, jumping up from *that* seat.

The woman in the dress sat back down in her seat. She pushed away the coffee cup that Hirai had drunk from and began reading her novel as if nothing had happened.

Hirai tried in vain to fix her tear-stained face. She let out a big sigh. 'I'm not sure they will welcome me back with open arms. And I wouldn't have a clue how to do the work . . .' she continued, looking down at Kumi's final letter in her hands.

'If I went back like this . . . it shouldn't be a problem, should it?'

It seemed that Hirai planned to return to Takakura immediately. Leaving the bar and everything else, just going. It was typical of Hirai to decide on something without feeling the need to think things over first. She had made up her mind and her face showed no trace of doubt.

Kei nodded reassuringly.

'I'm sure it'll be fine,' she answered cheerfully. She didn't ask Hirai what had happened in the past. She didn't need to. Hirai took out 380 yen from her purse to pay for the coffee. She gave it to Nagare and walked out of the cafe, light on her feet.

CLANG-DONG

Kei had walked out with Hirai to see her off. Now, she rubbed her stomach gently, and whispered, 'How wonderful was that . . .'

While Nagare was entering the coffee money into the cash register, he looked solemnly at Kei rubbing her stomach in that way.

I wonder if she can give it up?

Without Nagare's expression changing, the bell echoed throughout the cafe.

Clang . . . Dong . . .

IV

Mother and Child

_____

When it appears in haiku, the *higurashi* cicada is a term denoting the season, associated with autumn. The mention of the *higurashi*, therefore, evokes an image of it shrilling at the end of summer. In reality, this insect's cry can be heard from the beginning of summer. Somehow, though, while the shrills of the *abura* cicada and the *min-min* cicada evoke the images of a blazing sun, midsummer, and scorching days, the song of the *higurashi* evokes images of the evening and the late summer. When the sun begins to set and the dusk gathers, the *kana-kana-kana* of the *higurashi* evokes a melancholic mood, and one gets the urge to hurry home.

In the city, the shrill of the *higurashi* is seldom heard. This is because, unlike the *abura* cicada and the *min-min* cicada, the *higurashi* likes shady places such as the canopy of a forest, or of cypress groves away from the sun. But living near our cafe was a single *higurashi* cicada. When the sun started to set, a continual *kana-kana-kana* could be heard coming from

somewhere, shrilling fleetingly and weakly. This was sometimes audible in the cafe, though as the cafe was at basement level, you had to strain your ears to hear it – it was that
faint.

It was one such August evening. Outside, the *abura*
cicada was loudly shrilling, *jee jee jee*. The weather office had
reported that this day had been the hottest of the year. But
in the cafe, it was cool despite the lack of air conditioning.
Kazu was reading an email that Hirai had sent to Nagare's
phone.

> I have been back at Takakura for two weeks now. There
> are so many new things to learn. Every day I am nearly
> reduced to tears, it's so tough.

'Oh, she does have it tough . . .'
Listening to Kazu were Kohtake and Nagare. As neither
Kazu nor Kei had a phone, it was Nagare's phone that received
all emails sent to the cafe. Kazu didn't have a phone because
she was not very good at maintaining personal relationships,
and saw phones and means of communication as nothing
more than a nuisance. Kei didn't have a phone because she
cancelled it when she got married. *'One phone is enough for a
married couple,'* she said. In contrast, Hirai had three phones,
each for a particular purpose: for customers, for private, and
for family. On her family phone, she had saved only her family
home number, and her sister Kumi's number. Although no
one from the cafe knew it, now she had added two extra con-
tacts in her phone reserved for family: the cafe and Nagare's
mobile. Kazu continued to read out the email.

Things are still a bit awkward with my parents, but I feel returning home was for the best. I just think that if Kumi's death had led to unhappiness for both me and my parents, then that unhappiness would have been her only legacy.

So that's why I intend to lead a life that creates a more wonderful legacy for Kumi's life. I guess you never thought I could be so serious.

So anyway, I'm happy and well. If you get a chance please come and visit. Although it's already come and gone this year, I highly recommend the Tanabata Festival. Please send my regards to everyone.

Yaeko Hirai

Nagare, listening at the entrance to the kitchen with his arms folded, narrowed his eyes even more than usual. He was probably smiling – it was always difficult to know when he was smiling.

'Oh, isn't that wonderful,' Kohtake said, smiling happily. She must have been on a break between shifts as she was wearing her nurse's uniform. 'Hey, check out the photo,' Kazu said, showing Kohtake the photo attached to the email. Kohtake took the phone in her hands so that she could get a good look.

'Wow, she already looks the part . . . for sure,' she said, with a hint of surprise.

'Doesn't she!' Kazu agreed, smiling.

In the photo, Hirai was standing in front of the inn. With her hair in a bun, she was wearing a pink kimono, indicating her status as the owner of Takakura.

'She looks happy.'

'She does.'

Hirai was smiling like she didn't have a care in the world. She had written that things were still awkward between her and her parents but standing next to her were her father Yasuo and mother Michiko.

'And Kumi too . . .' muttered Nagare, peering at the photo from behind.

'Kumi's no doubt happy as well.'

'Yes, I'm sure she is,' Kohtake said, looking at the photo. Kazu standing beside her also gave a small nod. She no longer had the cool demeanour she had while conducting the ritual for returning to the past. Her face was gentle and kind.

'By the way,' Kohtake said as she returned the phone to Kazu. She turned and looked over dubiously to where the woman in the dress was sitting. 'What's she doing over there?'

It was not the woman in the dress she was looking at, but Fumiko Kiyokawa, who was sitting on the chair opposite her. It was Fumiko who had travelled back to the past in the cafe that spring. Normally the epitome of a working woman, today must have been her day off as she was dressed casually in a black T-shirt with three-quarter-length sleeves and white leggings. On her feet were cord sandals.

Fumiko had showed no interest in Hirai's email. Instead, she was staring at the face of the woman in the dress. Just what she wanted was a mystery. Kazu had no idea either.

'I wonder too,' was all that Kazu could reply.

Since spring, Fumiko had occasionally visited the cafe. When she did, she sat there opposite the woman in the dress.

Suddenly Fumiko looked at Kazu. 'Um, excuse me,' she said.

'Yes?'

'There is something that's been bothering me.'

'What is it?'

'This whole thing, where you get transported through time. Could you visit the future too?'

'The future?'

'Yes, the future.'

Hearing Fumiko's question, Kohtake's curiosity was piqued. 'Yes, I'd be interested to know that too.'

'I know, right?!' Fumiko agreed.

'Going back to the past or going to the future are both about being able to travel through time. So I thought maybe it's possible?' Fumiko continued.

Kohtake nodded in agreement.

'So is it possible?' Fumiko asked with eyes full of expectation and curiosity.

'Yeah, of course you can go to the future,' Kazu bluntly replied.

'Really?' Fumiko asked. Then in her excitement she accidentally bumped the table, spilling the woman in the dress's coffee. The woman twitched her eyebrows and in a great panic, Fumiko wiped the spilled coffee with a napkin – she didn't want to get cursed.

'Wow!' Kohtake exclaimed.

Kazu took in both women's responses. 'But no one goes,' she added coolly.

'What?' Fumiko asked, taken aback. 'Why on earth wouldn't they?' she demanded, drawing closer to Kazu. Surely she wasn't the only person to whom the idea of travelling to the future appealed – that's what she meant to say. Kohtake also looked as if she wanted to know why no one went. Her eyes widened and she looked intently at Kazu. Kazu looked to Nagare and then back at Fumiko.

'Well, OK . . . If you want to go to the future, how many years forward do you want to go?'

Despite the question apparently having come from nowhere, it seemed that Fumiko had already considered this.

'Three years from now!' Fumiko answered immediately, as if she had been waiting to be asked. Her face turned a little red.

'You want to meet your boyfriend?' Kazu enquired, apparently unmoved.

'Well . . . So what if I do?' She stuck out her jaw as if to defend herself, but her face grew redder.

At that point Nagare interrupted. 'No need to be embarrassed about it . . .'

'I'm nothing of the sort!' she retorted. But Nagare had touched a nerve, and both he and Kohtake were looking at each other, grinning.

Kazu was not in a teasing mood. She was looking at Fumiko with her usual cool expression. Fumiko picked up the seriousness.

'That's not possible?' she asked in a small voice.

'No, it's possible . . . It's not that it's not possible,' Kazu continued, in a flat monotone.

'But?'

'How can you know that in three years he will visit the cafe?'

Fumiko didn't appear to understand the point of the question.

'Don't you see?' Kazu asked Fumiko, as if cross-examining her.

'Oh,' Fumiko said, finally getting it. Even if she travelled forward in time by three years, how could she possibly be sure that Goro would be in the cafe?

'That's the sticking point. What's happened in the past has happened. You can target that moment and go back there. But . . .'

'The future is completely unknown!' Kohtake said, clapping her hands, as if playing on a quiz show.

'Sure, you can travel to the day you wish to go to, but there is no way of knowing if the person you want to meet is going to be there.'

Judging by Kazu's nonplussed expression, there must have been lots of other people who had pondered the same thing.

'So, unless you are counting on a miracle, if you decide on a time in the future and travel to it – for just that short time before the coffee cools – the chances of meeting the person you actually want to meet are very slim,' Nagare added, as if he explained this sort of thing all the time. He finished by looking at Fumiko with his narrow eyes asking, *You get what I'm saying?*

'So going would just be a waste of time?' Fumiko muttered with acceptance.

'Exactly.'

'I see . . .'

Considering how seemingly superficial her motive was, Fumiko probably should have been more embarrassed. But she was so impressed with the air-tight nature of the cafe's rules that it did not cross her mind to question Kazu's response further.

She didn't say anything but she thought to herself, *When you return to the past, you cannot change the present. Going to the future is simply a waste of time. How convenient. I can see why that magazine article described the cafe's time travel as 'meaningless'.*

But she wasn't going to avoid embarrassment so easily. Nagare further narrowed his eyes, inquisitively.

'What did you want to do? Make sure you were married?' he teased.

'Nothing of the sort!'

'Ha! Knew it.'

'No! I told you it's not that! . . . Ugh!'

The more she denied it, the deeper the hole Fumiko seemed to be digging herself into.

But unfortunately for her, she wouldn't have been able to travel to the future anyway. There was one more annoying rule preventing this from occurring: A person who has sat on the chair to travel through time once cannot do it a second time. Each person receives only a single chance.

But I think it would be easier not to tell Fumiko that, Kazu thought, as she observed Fumiko chatting happily. This was not out of consideration for Fumiko, but rather because she would demand a reasonable explanation for such a rule.

I can't be bothered dealing with that, Kazu thought simply.

CLANG-DONG

'Hello! Welcome!'

It was Fusagi. He was wearing a navy polo shirt, beige-brown trousers, and *setta* sandals. A bag hung from his shoulder. It was the hottest day of the year. In his hand, he held not a handkerchief but a small white towel, which he was using to wipe his sweat.

'Fusagi!' Nagare called his name rather than chanting the customer greeting of *Hello! Welcome!*

Fusagi first looked a bit confused, but then gave a small nod in reply and went to sit down at his usual seat, at the table closest to the entrance. Kohtake, with her hands behind her back, strolled up close to him.

'Hello, darling!' she said with a smile. She no longer called him Fusagi like she had used to.

'I'm sorry, do I know you?'

'I'm your wife, my love.'

'Wife? . . . My wife?'

'Yes.'

'This is a joke . . . Right?'

'No. I really am your wife!'

Without hesitation, she slipped into the seat facing him. Not sure how to react to this unknown woman behaving in such a familiar manner, he looked troubled.

'Er, I would prefer it if you didn't take the liberty of sitting there.'

'Oh, it's perfectly fine that I sit here . . . I'm your wife.'

'Um, it's not fine with me. I don't know you.'

'Well then, you'll have to get to know me. Let's start now.'

'What on earth do you mean?'

'Well, I guess it's a marriage proposal?'

While he was gaping at this woman in front of him, she sat there smiling. Visibly distressed, he sought the help of Kazu, who had come to serve him a glass of water.

'Um. Please could you do something about this woman?'

If you were a stranger taking a quick glance, you might see a couple in a good mood. But if you looked harder at Fusagi, you would see the face of a man in distress.

'He looks a bit upset,' Kazu said, offering him her support with a smile.

'Is he? . . . Oh well.'

'Maybe it's best to leave it at that for today?' Nagare said from behind the counter, offering a lifeboat.

Similar conversations had played out between the couple on several occasions. Some days, when Kohtake told Fusagi that she was his wife, he would refuse to believe it. But oddly on other days it was different. There would be times when he would say, '*Oh? Really?*' and accept it. Just two days earlier, she had sat opposite him and they had had what seemed to be an enjoyable conversation.

During such conversations they mainly talked about their memories of travel. Fusagi enjoyed telling her about how he had travelled here, or where he had visited there. She would look at him with a smile and add, '*I went there too,*' and both of them would become engrossed in the conversation. She had come to enjoy this kind of casual exchange.

'I guess so. I'll pick up the conversation when we get home,' she said and went back to sitting at the counter, resigned to leaving it at that for now.

'But you seem happy with things,' Nagare observed.

'Oh, I suppose.'

Despite the cool temperature of the cafe, Fusagi continued to wipe the sweat forming in beads on his face.

'Coffee, please,' he ordered as he removed the travel magazine from his shoulder bag and spread it out on the table.

'OK,' Kazu said with a smile, and disappeared into the kitchen. Fumiko once again began to stare at the woman in the dress. Kohtake was leaning forward with her cheeks resting on her hands and looking at Fusagi, who was looking down at the magazine, oblivious to the fact that he was being watched. Nagare, while watching these two, began to grind coffee using a retro-looking coffee mill. The woman in the dress, as always, continued to read her novel. As the aroma of freshly ground coffee filled the cafe, Kei appeared from the back room. The sight of her made Nagare stop.

'Good grief!' Kohtake said when she saw Kei's complexion. She looked very pale, almost bluish, and she was walking as if she might faint.

'Are you OK?' Nagare asked brusquely, clearly horrified as the blood seemed to have drained from his face too.

'Oh dear, sis, I think you'd better rest today,' Kazu called out from the kitchen.

'No, I'm OK. I'm fine,' Kei said, trying her hardest to look better, but she couldn't hide how unwell she was.

'You don't look like you're feeling too good today,' Kohtake said, standing up from her counter seat while assessing Kei's condition. 'You should be resting, don't you think?'

But Kei shook her head. 'No, I'm fine. Really,' she insisted, making a peace sign with her fingers.

But it was plain to see that she wasn't.

Kei was born with a weak heart. Ordered by doctors not to take part in intense physical activity, she was never able to take part in things like sports days when she was at school. Nevertheless, she was naturally sociable and free-spirited – an expert at enjoying life. This was one of 'Kei's talents for living happily', as Hirai would say.

If I am unable to do vigorous exercise, that's OK – I won't do vigorous exercise. That is how she thought.

Rather than just sitting out the races on sports days, she would get one of the boys to push her in a wheelchair. Of course they never had a chance of winning, but they gave it their all and always seemed to be bitterly disappointed when they lost. In dance class, she would make slow movements, in complete contrast to the swinging and shaking the others were doing. Doing things differently from everyone else would normally antagonize those making sure no one went against the grain, but no one ever thought that way with Kei. She was always everyone's friend; she had that sort of effect on people.

But irrespective of her strength of will or character, Kei's heart often seemed to deteriorate. Although never for very long, Kei was often pulled out of school and hospitalized for treatment. It was in hospital, in fact, that she met Nagare.

She was seventeen years old and in her second year of senior high school. While in hospital, she was confined to bed, so she got her enjoyment from the conversations she had with her visitors and the nurses who came into her room. She also enjoyed staring out at the outside world beyond her window. One day, while looking out the window, she saw in the hospital garden a man who was fully wrapped in bandages from head to toe.

She couldn't take her eyes off him. Not only was he entirely wrapped in bandages, but he was also so much bigger than everyone else. When a schoolgirl walked in front of him she appeared tiny by comparison. It was perhaps rude to do so, but Kei called him the *mummy man* and she could watch him all day without getting bored.

A nurse told her that the mummy man had been hospitalized after a traffic accident. He had been crossing the road at an intersection when there was a minor collision between a car and a truck just before his eyes. He luckily escaped the collision but the side of the truck dragged him about twenty metres and threw him into a shop window. The actual car crash was minor and the people in the car weren't injured. The truck, however, had driven up onto the kerb and toppled over. There were no other bystanders hurt. If the same thing had happened to someone of normal build, it could have meant sudden death, but the large man soon picked himself up as if nothing had happened. Of course, that was far from true, and he was a bloody mess, bleeding everywhere. But despite his condition, he stumbled to the overturned truck and called out, '*You OK?*' Petrol was leaking from the truck. The driver was unconscious. The big man pulled the driver from the truck and while casually carrying him over his shoulder called out to one of the onlookers gathered at the scene, '*Call an ambulance!*' When the ambulance came, they took the big man too. He had terrible bleeding from all the cuts and grazes, but he hadn't broken any bones.

After hearing the mummy man's background story, Kei grew even more intrigued. It wasn't long before this intrigue had grown into a full-blown crush. He became her first love. One day, on an impulse, she went to meet him. When she stood before him, he was even larger than she had imagined. It was like standing in front of a wall. 'I think you're the man I want to marry,' she declared, without reservations or embarrassment. She said it clearly and directly to the mummy man – the first words she had ever spoken to him.

The mummy man looked down at her and for a while said nothing. Then he offered a pragmatic yet not entirely negative reply.

'You'll be working in a cafe if you do.'

Their three years of dating started then, and finally when Kei was twenty and Nagare was twenty-three, they signed the registry books and became husband and wife.

Kei went behind the counter and began drying the dishes and putting them away, as she always did. The siphon could be heard beginning to gurgle from the kitchen. Kohtake continued to look at Kei with concern, but Kazu slipped into the kitchen and Nagare once again started grinding coffee beans with the mill. For some reason, unbeknownst to everyone, the woman in the dress was continuing to stare at Kei.

'Oh,' Kohtake exclaimed just before the sound of breaking glass could be heard.

The glass had fallen from Kei's hand.

'Sis! Are you OK?' Normally so calm and collected under any circumstances, Kazu came rushing out in a panic.

'I'm sorry,' Kei said, beginning to pick up the broken glass.

'Leave it, Sis, I'll do it,' Kazu said while propping up Kei, who was beginning to buckle at the knees.

Nagare said nothing and watched.

It was the first time Kohtake had seen Kei in such a serious condition. Being a nurse, she dealt with ill people all the time. But seeing her friend looking so unwell shook her to the point of the blood draining from her face.

'Kei, darling,' she muttered,

'Are you OK?' asked Fumiko.

It naturally caught Fusagi's attention as well, and he lifted his head.

'I'm sorry.'

'I think Kei should go to the hospital,' Kohtake advised.

'No, I'll be OK, really . . .'

'But I really think . . .'

Kei shook her head stubbornly. But her chest was heaving as she breathed. Her condition seemed worse than she thought.

Nagare said nothing. He just kept looking sombrely at his wife.

Kei took a deep breath. 'I think I had better lie down,' she said and staggered towards the back room. She had gathered from Nagare's expression that he was seriously concerned about her condition.

'Kazu, look after the cafe, please,' Nagare said as he followed her.

'Yeah, sure,' Kazu replied, standing still as if her mind was elsewhere.

'Coffee, please.'

'Oh! . . . Sorry.'

Fusagi obviously had read the mood and had been biting his tongue, waiting to make his request. His prompt for coffee brought Kazu back from her daze. She had been so caught up with Kei, she still hadn't served Fusagi his coffee.

The day ended with this heavy mood still lingering.

Since becoming pregnant, whenever she was free, Kei would talk to the baby. At four weeks, it was a bit early to be calling it a baby, but that didn't deter her. In the morning she would start with 'good morning', and while calling Nagare 'Papa', she would set out to explain the events of the day. She found these imaginary conversations with her baby the highlight of any day.

'Can you see? It's your papa!'

'My father?'

'*Yes!*'

'He's huge!'

'Yes, but he doesn't only have a huge body. He has a huge heart as well! He is a very kind, loving papa.'

'That's good! I can't wait.'

'Papa and Mama can't wait to see you either, my love!'

So went these conversations in which – of course – Kei played both roles. But the sad reality was that Kei's condition was worsening as her pregnancy progressed. At five weeks, a sac has formed inside the uterus and inside *there* is the embryo, measuring one or two millimetres. This is when the baby's heartbeat becomes detectable. From this point organs begin to form quickly: eyes, ears, and mouth develop; the stomach, intestines, lungs, pancreas, cerebral nerves, and aorta are formed; the hands and feet begin to protrude. All this early foetal development was taking a toll on Kei's physical condition.

She was also getting hot flushes yet felt like she had a fever. The hormones that her body was producing in order to create the placenta were making her feel lethargic and subject to strong waves of sudden drowsiness. The pregnancy affected her mood, which would swing from one extreme to another. She would have periods of anxiety, short bursts of anger, and then feel depressed. There were times when some things seemed to taste different from normal.

Despite this, however, she never once complained. Conditioned by her regular spells in hospital since childhood, she never complained about her physical ailments.

But over the course of the last couple of days, her condition had rapidly grown worse. Two days earlier, Nagare had taken advantage of a brief moment alone with her primary doctor to demand more information. The doctor had confided in him.

'Frankly, your wife's heart may be unable to withstand childbirth. Morning sickness will begin from the sixth week. If she gets a bad bout of morning sickness, she will need to be hospitalized. If she chooses to have the baby, she has to realize that the possibility that both she and her child will survive is very low. Even if she and her baby survive the birth, it would take a tremendous toll on her body. She must understand that it will definitely reduce her lifespan.'

He added, 'Normally, terminations are performed between six and twelve weeks. In your wife's case, should she choose to end the pregnancy, it should be done as early as possible . . .'

After returning home, Nagare confronted Kei, telling her everything that had been said. After he had finished, Kei simply nodded.

'*I know*,' was all she said.

After closing the cafe, Nagare sat alone at the counter. The room was lit only by the wall lamps. On the counter, several small paper cranes were lined up – made by Nagare from a folded paper napkin. The only sound that could be heard inside the cafe was the ticking of the wall clocks. The only things moving were Nagare's hands.

CLANG-DONG

Although the bell rang out, Nagare showed no reaction. He just placed the paper crane he had finished folding on the counter with the rest. Kohtake walked into the cafe. She had dropped by on her way home from work because she was worried about Kei.

Nagare, who was staring at the paper cranes on the counter, nodded his head slightly.

Kohtake stood at the cafe's entrance. 'How's Kei doing?' she asked. She had found out that she was pregnant early on, but she had never thought it would cause her to deteriorate so rapidly. She looked just as worried as she had earlier that day.

Nagare didn't answer straight away. He took a single napkin and began folding it.

'She's managing somehow,' he said.

Kohtake sat down at the counter leaving a seat between them.

Nagare scratched the tip of his nose. 'Sorry to cause so much worry,' he said, nodding apologetically as he looked over at her.

'You don't have to worry about that . . . but shouldn't she be in hospital?'

'I told her she should, but she won't listen.'

'Yes, but . . .'

He finished folding the paper crane and stared at it.

'I was against her having the baby,' he muttered in a faint voice. If the cafe hadn't been so small and quiet, Kohtake wouldn't have heard it. 'But nothing will change her mind,' he said, looking at Kohtake with a slight smile and then looking down.

He had told Kei that he 'was against' their having the baby but that was as far as he would go. He could say neither 'Don't have it' nor 'I want you to have it.' He couldn't choose between them, choosing Kei over the baby or choosing the baby over Kei.

Kohtake didn't know what to say. She looked up at the ceiling fan that was rotating gently.

'That's tough,' she agreed.

Kazu came out from the back room.

'Kazu . . .' Kohtake whispered.

But Kazu averted her gaze from Kohtake and looked at Nagare. She wasn't her normal unreadable self: she seemed sad and despondent.

'How is she?' Nagare asked.

Kazu looked towards the back room. Nagare followed her eyes and saw Kei slowly approaching. Her complexion was still white and she walked a little unsteadily, but she seemed to be in much more control. She walked behind the counter and stood in front of Nagare looking at him, but he didn't look back. Instead, he simply stared at the paper cranes on the counter. As neither Nagare nor Kei spoke, the silence between them grew more awkward by the minute. Kohtake felt unable to move.

Kazu went into the kitchen and began to make coffee. She placed the filter in the funnel and poured hot water from the kettle into the flask. As everything was so quiet in the cafe, it was easy to tell what she was doing, even though she was out of sight. Soon the contents of the flask began to boil, and a gurgling sound of hot water ascending the funnel could be heard. After a few minutes the aroma of fresh coffee filled the cafe. As if roused by the aroma, Nagare looked up.

'I'm sorry, Nagare,' Kei mumbled.

'What for?' Nagare asked, staring at the paper cranes.

'I'll go to the hospital tomorrow.'

'. . .'

'I'll get admitted.' Kei said each word to herself as if trying to make peace with something she was still wrestling with. 'To be honest, once I go into hospital, I don't imagine I'll ever come home again. It's a decision I have been unable to make . . .'

'I see.' Nagare clenched his fists tightly.

Kei lifted her chin and stared with her large round eyes into space. 'But it seems I can't go on like this any longer,' she said as her eyes filled with tears.

Nagare listened quietly.

'There's only so much my body can take . . .'

Kei placed her hands on her stomach, which had yet to expand even an inch. 'It looks like giving birth to this child will take my all . . .' she said with a knowing smile. It seemed that when it came to her body, she knew better than anyone.

'That's why . . .'

Nagare looked at her with his narrow eyes. 'OK,' was all that he could reply. 'Kei, darling . . .'

This was the first time that Kohtake had seen Kei upset like this. As a nurse, she understood the real danger that she faced in attempting to bear a baby with her heart condition. Her body had already become this frail while she was still just approaching the morning sickness phase. If she had chosen not to have the baby, no one would have blamed her, but she had decided to go ahead.

'But I'm really scared,' Kei muttered in a trembling voice. 'I wonder if my child will be happy.'

'Will Mama's baby be lonely? Will that make you cry?' She talked to the child as she always did. 'I might only be able to have you, my child. Will you forgive me?'

She listened, but no answer came.

A stream of tears flowed down her cheek.

'I'm scared . . . the thought of not being there for my child is frightening,' she said, looking directly at Nagare. 'I don't know what I should do. I want my child to be happy. How can such a simple wish be so terribly scary?' she cried.

Nagare gave no reply. He just gazed at the paper cranes on the counter.

Flap.

The woman in the dress closed her novel. She hadn't finished it: a white bookmark with a red ribbon tied to it was left inserted between the pages. Hearing the book close, Kei looked over at her. The woman in the dress looked back at Kei and just went on staring at her.

With her eyes fixed on Kei, the woman in the dress gently blinked just once. Then she smoothly got up from her seat. It was as if that blink had been meant to communicate something, yet she walked behind Nagare and Kohtake and disappeared into the toilet as if she was being drawn inside.

Her seat – *that* seat – was vacant.

Kei started walking towards the seat as if something was pulling her there. Then once in front of *that* seat – the one that can send you to the past – she stood staring at it.

'Kazu . . . could you make some coffee, please?' she called weakly.

Hearing Kei's request, Kazu poked her head from the kitchen and saw her standing next to that seat. She had no idea what was on Kei's mind.

Nagare turned round and saw Kei's back. 'Oh, come on . . . You're not serious?' he said.

Kazu spotted that the woman in the dress was gone, and remembered the conversation from earlier that day. Fumiko Kiyokawa had asked, 'Could you visit the future too?'

Fumiko's wish was simple: she wanted to know whether or not in three years, Goro had returned from America and they were married. Kazu had said that it could be done but that no one decided to go because it was pointless. But that was exactly what Kei wanted to do.

'Just one look is all I want.'

'Hang on.'

'If I could see, for just a moment, that would be enough . . .'

'Do you seriously intend on going to the future?' Nagare asked, his tone gruffer than usual.

'It's all I can do . . .'

'But you don't know if you can meet?'

'. . .'

'What's the point of going there if you don't meet?'

'I understand that, but . . .'

Kei looked pleadingly into Nagare's eyes.

But Nagare could only produce one word. 'No,' he said. He turned his back on Kei and withdrew into silence.

Nagare had never before stood in the way of Kei doing anything. He respected her insistent and determined personality. He didn't even argue strongly against her decision to put her life on the line to have a child. But he objected to this.

He wasn't just concerned with whether or not she would have her child. He thought that if she went into the future and discovered that the child didn't exist, the inner strength that had been sustaining her would be destroyed.

Kei stood before the chair, weak but desperate. She couldn't walk away from her decision. She was not going to retreat from her position in front of that chair.

'I need you to decide how many years into the future,' Kazu said suddenly. She slid beside her and cleared away the cup that the woman in the dress had been drinking from.

'How many years? And what month, date, and time?' she asked Kei. She looked directly into Kei's eyes and gave a small nod.

'Kazu!' Nagare shouted with all the authority he could muster. But Kazu ignored him and with her trademark cool expression said, 'I will remember. I will make sure you can meet . . .'

'Kazu, sweetheart.'

Kazu was promising her that she would make sure her child would be there in the cafe at the time that she chose to go to in the future. 'So you don't have to worry,' she said.

Kei gazed into her eyes and gave a little nod.

Kazu had a feeling that the deterioration in Kei's condition over the past few days wasn't down to the physical changes from the pregnancy alone, but that it had also been caused by the overall stress of the situation. Kei wasn't afraid to die. Her anxiety and sadness stemmed from the thought of not being there to see her child grow up. This weighed heavily on her heart, and was sapping her physical strength. As her strength faded, her sense of anxiety grew. Negativity is food for a malady, one might say. Kazu feared that if Kei continued on this course, her condition would continue to weaken as the pregnancy progressed and the lives of both mother and child might be lost.

A glimmer of positivity returned to Kei's eyes.

I can meet my child.

It was a very, very small hope. Kei turned to look at Nagare sitting at the counter. Her eyes locked with his.

He was silent for a moment but with a short sigh, he turned away. 'Do as you wish,' he said, turning on his stool so that his back was to her.

'Thank you,' she said to his back.

After making sure that Kei was able to slide in between the table and the seat, Kazu took the cup that the woman in the dress had used and disappeared into the kitchen. Kei inhaled deeply, slowly lowered herself into the seat, and closed her eyes. Kohtake held her hands together in front of her as if in prayer, while Nagare stared silently at the paper cranes in front of him.

This was the first time Kei had seen Kazu defy Nagare's will. Outside the cafe, Kazu rarely felt comfortable talking with anyone she hadn't met before. She went to Tokyo University of the Arts, but Kei had never seen her with anyone you might describe as a friend. She normally kept to herself. When not in university, she helped out at the cafe, and when that was finished, she retired to her room, where she would work on her drawings.

Kazu's drawings were hyper-realist. Using only pencils, she created works that appeared as true to life as actual photographs, but she could only draw things she could observe herself; her drawings never depicted the imaginary or the invented. People don't see things and hear things as objectively as they might think. The visual and auditory information that enters the mind is distorted by experiences, thoughts, circumstances, wild fancies, prejudices, preferences, knowledge, awareness, and countless other workings of the mind. Pablo Picasso's sketch of a nude man that he did at age eight is remarkable. The painting he did at age fourteen of a Catholic communion ceremony is very realistic. But later, after the shock of his best friend's suicide, he created paintings in shades of blue that became known as the Blue Period. Then he met a new lover and created the bright and colourful works of the Rose Period. Influenced by African sculptures, he became part of the cubist movement. Then he turned to a neoclassical style, continued on to surrealism, and eventually painted the famous works *The Weeping Woman* and *Guernica*.

Taken together, these artworks show the world as seen through Picasso's eyes. They are the result of something passing through the filter that is Picasso. Until now, Kazu had never sought to challenge or influence people's opinions or behaviour. This was because her own feelings didn't form part of the filter through which she interacted with the world. Whatever happened, she tried not to influence it by keeping herself at a safe distance. That was Kazu's place – it was her way of life.

This was how she treated everyone. Her cool disposition when handling customers wishing to go back to the past was her way of saying, 'Your reasons for going back to the past are none of my business.' But this was different. She had made a promise. She was encouraging Kei to go to the future, and her actions were having a direct influence on Kei's future. It crossed Kei's mind that Kazu must have her reasons for her out-of-character behaviour, but those reasons were not immediately apparent.

'Sis.' Kei opened her eyes to Kazu's voice. Standing next to the table, Kazu was holding a silver tray upon which was set a white coffee cup and a small silver kettle.

'Are you OK?'

'Yes, I'm fine.'

Kei corrected her posture and Kazu quietly placed the coffee cup in front of her.

How many years from now? she prompted silently with a small tilt of the head. Kei thought for a moment.

'I want to make it ten years, on 27 August,' she declared.

When Kazu heard the date, she gave a little smile.

'OK then,' she replied. 27 August was Kei's birthday: a date that neither Kazu nor Nagare would forget. 'And the time?'

'Three in the afternoon,' Kei replied instantly.

'In ten years from now, on 27 August, at three in the afternoon.'

'Yes, please,' Kei said, smiling.

Kazu gave a small nod and gripped the handle of the silver kettle. 'Right, then.' She resumed her normal cool persona.

Kei looked over at Nagare. 'See you soon,' she called, sounding clear-minded.

He didn't look back. 'Yeah, OK.'

During Kei and Nagare's exchange, Kazu picked up the kettle and held it still above the coffee cup.

'Drink the coffee before it goes cold,' she whispered.

The words sounded throughout the silent cafe. Kei could feel the tension in the room.

Kazu began pouring the coffee. A narrow, black stream flowed from the small opening of the kettle's spout, slowly filling the cup. Kei's gaze was fixed not on the cup but on Kazu. When the coffee had reached the top, Kazu noticed her gaze and smiled warmly as if to say, '*I will make sure you will meet . . .*'

A shimmering plume of steam rose from the full cup of coffee. Kei felt her body shimmering as if it were steam. In a moment, she had become as light as a cloud and everything around her had begun to flow as if she were in the middle of a film playing on fast-forward.

Normally she would have reacted to this by gazing at the passing scenery with the sparkly eyes of a child at an amusement park. But such was her mood right now that her mind was closed even from appreciating such a weird experience. Nagare had put his foot down in opposition, but Kazu had stepped up to give her a chance. Now she was waiting to meet her child. Surrendering to the shimmering dizziness, she brought to mind her own childhood.

Kei's father, Michinori Matsuzawa, also had a weak heart. He collapsed at work while Kei was in grade three at elementary school. After that, he was frequently in and out of hospital, until he departed just one year later. Kei was nine years old, a naturally sociable child who was always happy and smiling.

And yet at the same time, she was sensitive and highly strung. Her father's death left her in a dark place emotionally. She had encountered death for the first time, and referred to it as the very dark box. Once you climbed inside that box, you never got out. Her father was trapped in there – a place where you encountered no one, awful and lonely. When she thought of her father, her nights were robbed of sleep. Gradually, her smile faded.

Her mother Tomako's reaction to her husband's death was the opposite of Kei's. She spent her days with a permanent smile. She had never really had a bright disposition. She and Michinori seemed an unexciting and ordinary married couple. Tomako had cried at the funeral but after that day, she never showed a miserable face. She smiled far more than she had done before. Kei couldn't understand at all why her mother was always smiling. She asked her, 'Why are you so happy when Dad is dead? Aren't you sad?'

Tomako, who knew that Kei described death as the very dark box, answered, 'Well, if your father could see us from that very dark box, what do you suppose he would be thinking?'

With nothing but the kindest of thoughts for Kei's father, Tomako was trying her best to answer the accusatory question that Kei was asking: '*Why are you so happy?*'

'You father didn't go in that box because he wanted to. There was a reason. He had to go. If your father could see from his box and see you crying every day, what do you think he would think? I think it would make him sad. You know how much your father loved you. Don't you think it would be painful for him to see the unhappy face of someone he loved? So why don't you smile every day so that your father can smile from his box? Our smiles allow him to smile. Our happiness allows your father to be happy in his box.' On hearing this explanation, Kei's eyes welled up with tears.

Hugging Kei tightly, Tomako's eyes glistened with the tears that she had kept hidden since the funeral.

Next it will be my turn to go into the box . . .

Kei understood for the first time how hard it must have been for her father. Her heart tightened at the thought of how devastated he must have been, knowing that his time was up and that he had to leave his family. But by finally taking into account her father's feelings, she also understood more fully the greatness of her mother's words. She realized that only a deep love and understanding of her husband would have allowed her mother to say those things.

After a while, everything around her gradually slowed and settled. She transformed from steam back into bodily form, changing shape back into Kei.

Thanks to Kazu, she had arrived – ten years in the future. The first thing she did was to look around the room carefully.

The thick wall pillars and the wooden beam crossing the ceiling were a lustrous dark brown, the colour of chestnuts. On the walls were the three large wall clocks. The tan walls were made of earthen plaster with the patina left by more than one hundred years; she thought it was wonderful. The dim lighting that coloured the entire cafe with a sepia hue – even during the day – gave no sense of time. The retro atmosphere of the cafe had a comforting effect. Above, there was a wooden ceiling fan, rotating slowly without a sound. There was nothing to tell her that she had arrived ten years into the future.

However, the tear-off calendar next to the cash register showed that it was indeed 27 August, and Kazu, Nagare, and Kohtake, who had been in the cafe with her until moments ago, were now nowhere to be seen.

In their place, a man stood behind the counter, staring at her.

She was confused to see him. He was wearing a white shirt, black waistcoat, and bow tie, and he had a standard, short-back-and-sides hairstyle. It was clear that he worked in the cafe. He was standing behind the counter for one thing, and he didn't appear surprised that Kei had just suddenly appeared in the chair, so he must have known about the special nature of the seat she was sitting in.

He did not say anything, just kept staring at Kei. To not engage with the person who had appeared was precisely how a staff member would behave. After a while, the man began squeakily polishing the glass he was holding. He looked as if he was in his late thirties, maybe early forties – he just looked like a standard-issue waiter. He didn't have the friendliest of manners, and there was a large burn scar running from above his right eyebrow to his right ear, which gave him a rather intimidating air.

'Um, excuse me . . .'

Normally Kei wasn't the type to worry whether a person was approachable or not. She could begin a conversation with anyone and address them as if they had been friends for years. But at that moment she was feeling a little confused by everything. She spoke to the man as if she was a foreigner struggling with a second language.

'Um, where's the manager?'

'The manager?'

'The cafe manager, is he here?'

The man behind the counter returned the polished glass to the shelf.

'That would be me, I guess . . .' he replied.

'What?'

'I'm sorry, what is it?'

'You are? You're the manager?'

'Yes.'

'Of here?'

'Yes.'

'Of this cafe?'

'Yes.'

'Really?'

'Yep.'

That can't be right! Kei leaned back in surprise.

The man behind the counter was startled by her response. He stopped what he was doing and came out from behind the counter. 'What – what's wrong, exactly?' he said, clearly rattled. Perhaps it was the first time someone had reacted in such a way to learning he was the manager. But Kei's expression seemed over the top.

Kei was trying hard to make sense of the situation. What had happened during these ten years? She couldn't work out how this could be. She had so many questions for the man in front of her, but her thoughts were a jumble and time was of the essence. The coffee would go cold and her decision to come to the future would have been in vain.

She collected herself. She looked up at the man, who was peering at her with concern.

I must calm myself . . .

'Um . . .'

'Yes?'

'What about the previous manager?'

'Previous manager?'

'You know. Really big guy, narrow eyes . . .'

'Oh, Nagare . . .'

'Right!'

The man at least knew Nagare. Kei found herself leaning forward.

'Nagare is in Hokkaido right now.'

'Hokkaido . . .'

'Yes.'

She blinked in amazement, she needed to hear it a second time. 'Huh? Hokkaido?'

'Yes.'

She began to feel dizzy. It wasn't going as she had planned. Since she had known Nagare, never once had he mentioned anything about Hokkaido.

'But why?'

'Well, that I can't answer,' the man said as he rubbed the skin above his right eyebrow.

She felt utterly rattled. Nothing was making sense.

'Oh, was it your plan to meet Nagare?'

Unaware of Kei's mission, the man had guessed wrongly, but she had lost the will to answer. It was all futile. She was never very good at thinking about things rationally; she always made her decisions in life guided by intuition. So when faced with a situation like this, she was at a loss to understand what was going on, or how it could have happened. She had thought that if she could go to the future, she could meet her child. As her mood began to sink, the man asked, 'Then, you came to meet Kazu?'

'Aha!' Kei shouted, suddenly seeing new hope.

How could she have forgotten! She had focused on asking the man about the *manager*, but she had forgotten something important: it was Kazu who had encouraged her to go to the future; it was she who had made the promise. It didn't matter if Nagare was in Hokkaido. As long as Kazu was here, there was no problem. Kei tried to contain her surging excitement.

'What about Kazu?' she quickly asked.

'What?'

'Kazu! Is Kazu here?'

If the man had been standing any closer, Kei probably would have grabbed him by his shirt front.

Her intensity compelled him to take a couple of steps back.

'Is she here or not?'

'Um, look . . .' The man averted his gaze, overwhelmed by Kei's quick-fire questioning.

'The truth is . . . Kazu is in Hokkaido as well,' the man replied carefully.

That's it then . . . The man's reply had completely dashed her hopes.

'Oh no, not even Kazu is here?'

He looked with concern at Kei. She looked as if her spirit had been totally sapped from her.

'Are you all right?' he asked.

Kei looked up at the man with a look that said, *'Isn't it perfectly obvious?'* but he had no idea about her situation, and so there was nothing she could say.

'Yeah, I'm fine . . .' she said dejectedly.

The man tilted his head in confusion and walked back behind the counter.

Kei began rubbing her stomach.

I don't know why, but if those two are in Hokkaido, then this child must be with them there too . . . It doesn't look like it's going to happen.

She dropped her shoulders, slumping despondently. It was always going to be a gamble. If luck was on her side, they would meet. Kei had known that. If meeting people in the future was so easy, then more people would be trying it.

For example, if Fumiko Kiyokawa and Goro had promised to meet at the cafe in three years' time, then of course, it was possible they would meet. But for this to happen, Goro would have to keep his promise to come. There were many reasons for being unable to keep such a promise. He could try to drive but get stuck in traffic, or he could decide to walk but get diverted by roadworks. He might get stopped and asked for directions, or lose his way. There might even be a sudden torrential downpour or a natural disaster. He might sleep in or simply mix up the time they were due to meet. In other words, the future is uncertain.

With this in mind, whatever the reason for Nagare and Kazu being in Hokkaido, it fell within the range of things that can happen. Hokkaido was a thousand kilometres away and it was a shock to hear they had gone so far. But even if they'd only been one train stop away, they would still have been unable to get back to the cafe before the coffee went cold.

Suppose when she returned to the present, she conveyed this turn of events, it would not change the fact that they were in Hokkaido – Kei knew the rule. Her luck had run out. It was as simple as that. After thinking things over, she began to feel more collected. She picked up the cup and took a sip. The coffee was still pretty warm. She could switch moods quickly: another one of her talents for living happily. Her ups and downs could be extreme, but they never lingered. It was a shame that she couldn't meet her child, but she had no regrets. She had followed her wishes and had managed to travel to the future. She wasn't cross with Kazu or Nagare either. They surely had a good reason. It was inconceivable that they wouldn't have done their best to be there to meet her.

For me, the promise was made just a few minutes ago. Here, it is ten years later. Oh well . . . it can't be helped. When I go back, I may as well say that we met . . .

Kei reached out for the sugar pot sitting on the table.

CLANG-DONG

Just as she was planning to add sugar to her coffee, the bell rang, and out of habit, she was about to yell, *'Hello, welcome!'* when the man said it before her.

Kei bit her lip and looked over to the entrance.

'Oh, it's you,' the man called.

'Hi, I'm back,' said a girl who looked like she might be in junior high school, fourteen or fifteen years old. She was wearing summer clothes: a sleeveless white shirt with cropped denim trousers and cord sandals. Her hair was neatly done up in a ponytail fastened with a red hairclip.

Oh . . . the girl from the other day.

Kei recognized her as soon as she saw her face. It was the girl who had come from the future and asked to have their photo taken together. She was wearing winter clothes at the time, and had her hair cut short, so she looked a little different. But Kei remembered how she had been struck by those big sweet eyes.

So this is where we meet.

Kei nodded in understanding, and folded her arms. On that occasion, she had thought it weird to have a visitor she didn't recognize, but now it made sense.

'We had a photo taken together, didn't we?' she said to the girl.

But the girl's face showed a puzzled expression.

'I'm sorry, what are you talking about?' she asked tentatively.

Kei realized her error.

Oh, I see . . .

The girl must come after this meeting. Her question obviously wouldn't make any sense in that case.

'Oh, forget I said that, it's nothing,' she said smiling to the girl. But the girl seemed unnerved. She gave a polite little nod and disappeared into the back room.

Well, that makes me feel better.

Kei felt much happier now. She had come to the future only to find Kazu and Nagare gone and in their place a man she didn't recognize. She had begun to feel depressed at the prospect of returning home with nothing having turned out as she'd imagined. But that all changed when the girl appeared.

She touched her cup to check that it was still warm.

We must become friends before this coffee cools.

Thinking this, a heartening feeling of elation filled her chest – an encounter between people ten years apart.

The girl came back into the cafe.

Oh . . .

She was holding a wine-red apron.

That's the apron I used!

Kei hadn't forgotten her original aim. But she wasn't the type to stew over things that weren't going to happen. She altered her plan: she would befriend this interesting girl. The man peered out from the kitchen and glanced at the girl with the apron.

'Oh, you don't have to help out today. After all . . . There's just that one customer.'

But the girl gave no reply and stood behind the counter.

The man didn't seem intent on pressing the issue and withdrew into the kitchen. The girl began to wipe the counter.

Hey! Look this way!

Kei was desperately trying to attract the girl's attention by rocking her body left and right, but the girl didn't look up at her once. This did not douse Kei's enthusiasm.

If she is helping here, perhaps that means she is the manager's daughter?

Kei considered such possibilities.

Beep-boop beep-boop . . . Beep-boop beep-boop

The disruptive sound of a phone ringing could be heard from the back room.

'I've . . .' Kei suddenly fought the hard-wired response to answer the phone. It may have been ten years later but the sound of a phone was unchanged.

Oh . . . Be careful . . . That was close . . .

She almost broke the rule and left the seat. She was able to leave the seat but if so would have been forcefully returned to the present.

The man came out from the kitchen calling, 'I've got it,' and went into the back room to answer the phone. Kei made an exaggerated gesture of wiping her brow and gave a sigh of relief. She heard the man talking.

'Yes, hello? Oh hi! Yes, she is . . . Oh, right. OK, hang on. I'll get her . . .'

The man suddenly came out from the back room.

Hmm?

The man brought the phone to Kei.

'Phone,' he said as he handed Kei the handset.

'For me?'

'It's Nagare.'

On hearing Nagare's name, she promptly took the phone.

'Hello! Why are you in Hokkaido? Can you explain to me what's going on?' she said, in a voice loud enough to resound throughout the cafe.

The man, still not grasping the situation, tilted his head in confusion and returned to the kitchen.

The girl showed no response, as if she was oblivious to Kei's loud voice. She simply continued doing what she was doing.

'What's that? There's no time? I'm the one with no time!' Even as she was talking the coffee was cooling. 'I can hardly hear you! What?' She was holding the handset to her left ear while plugging her right ear with her other hand. For some reason, there was a terrible racket in the background on the other end of the line which made it difficult to hear anything.

'What? A schoolgirl?' She continued to get Nagare to repeat what he was saying. 'Yes, she's here. The one who visited the cafe about two weeks ago; she came from the future to get a photo with me. Yes, yes. What about her?' she asked looking at the girl, who, while averting her gaze, had stopped what she was doing.

I wonder why she looks so nervous? Kei thought as the conversation continued. It was bothering her, but she had to focus on listening to the important information Nagare was giving her.

'Like I told you, I can hardly hear what you're saying. Eh? What? That girl?'

Our daughter.

Just at that moment, the middle wall clock began to chime, *dong, dong* . . . ten times.

It was then that Kei first realized what the time was. The time she had arrived at in the future was not three in the afternoon. It was ten in the morning. The smile fell from her face.

'Oh, OK. Right,' she replied in a weak voice. She hung up and placed the handset on the table.

She had been looking forward to speaking to the girl. But now her expression was pale and drawn, without any remnants of that bright expectant look that existed just moments before. The girl had stopped what she was doing and also looked completely spooked. Kei slowly reached out and held the cup to check the temperature of the coffee. It was still warm. There was time left before it was completely cold.

She turned and looked at the girl again.

My child . . .

The realization that she was now face to face with her child hit her suddenly. The static had made the phone call difficult to hear but she had got the gist of it.

You planned to travel ten years into the future, but there was some kind of mistake and you travelled fifteen years. It seems ten years 15.00 and fifteen years 10.00 were mixed up. We heard about it when you returned from the future but right now, we are in Hokkaido for unavoidable reasons that I won't go into because there's no time. The girl you see before you is our daughter. You don't have much time left, so just have a good look at our all-grown-up, fit-and-well daughter and go home.

After having said all that, Nagare must have been worried about the time Kei had left, and he simply hung up on her. Having learned that the girl in front of her was her daughter, Kei suddenly had no idea how to talk to her.

More than confusion and panic, she felt a strong sense of regret.

What she regretted was pretty simple. She was in no doubt that the girl knew she was her mother. But Kei had assumed the girl was someone else's daughter – the age difference had been too big. Although she didn't pay any attention to it until now, Kei suddenly heard the sound of the ticking hands of the wall clocks. They seemed to be saying, 'Tick-tock tick-tock, the coffee is going cold!' There was indeed no time.

But Kei saw in the girl's sullen expression an answer to the question she wanted to ask but hadn't managed to: *Can you forgive me that all I could do was to bring you into this world?* and it cast a shadow over her heart. She struggled to think what to say.

'What's your name?' she asked.

But without responding to the simple question, the girl bowed her head in silence.

Kei interpreted this as further proof that she blamed her. Unable to bear the silence, she also bowed her head. Then . . .

'Miki . . .' The girl offered her name in a small, sad, and weak-sounding voice.

Kei wanted to ask so much. But from hearing how faint Miki's voice was, she got the impression that she was reluctant to speak to her.

'Miki, oh, that's nice . . .' was all she managed in response.

Miki said nothing. Instead, she looked at Kei as if she didn't like her reaction and rushed towards the back room. At that moment, the man poked his head out from the kitchen.

'Miki, are you OK?' he called, but Miki ignored him and vanished into the back room.

CLANG-DONG

'Hello, welcome!'

A woman entered the cafe just as the man offered his greeting. She was wearing a short-sleeved white blouse, black trousers, and a wine-red apron. She must have been running in the hot sun as she was out of breath and sweating profusely.

'Ah!' Kei recognized her. Or at least, she was still recognizable.

Looking at the panting woman, though, Kei got a real sense that fifteen years had passed. It was Fumiko Kiyokawa, the woman who just earlier that day had asked Kei if she was OK. Fumiko had had a slim build then but now she was quite round.

Fumiko noticed that Miki wasn't there. 'Where is Miki?' she asked the man.

She must have known that Kei was going to come at this time today. She had that sense of urgency. The man was obviously flustered by her tone.

'In the back,' he answered. He still didn't understand what was going on.

'Why?' she asked as she slapped her hand on the counter.

'What?' he said unapologetically. He started rubbing the scar above his right eyebrow, confused as to why he was being blamed.

'I don't believe this,' she sighed, glaring at the man. But she didn't want to waste time on accusations. She was already at fault for being late for such an important event.

'So you're looking after the cafe?' Kei asked in a weak voice.

'Uh, yeah,' Fumiko answered, looking directly at her. 'Did you talk to Miki?'

It was a straightforward enough question that Kei felt uncomfortable answering. She just looked down.

'Did you have a proper talk?' Fumiko pressed.

'Oh, I don't know . . .' Kei mumbled.

'I'll go and call her.'

'No, it's OK!' Kei said more clearly, halting Fumiko, who was already making her way to the back room.

'Why do you say that?'

'It's enough,' Kei said with a struggle. 'We saw each other's faces.'

'Oh, come on.'

'She didn't seem like she wanted to meet . . .'

'Oh, she does so!' Fumiko said, contradicting Kei. 'Miki has really wanted to meet you. She has been looking forward to this day for so long . . .'

'I just think I must have caused her so much sadness.'

'Of course there have been times when she's been down.'

'I thought as much . . .'

Kei reached out for the coffee cup. Fumiko saw her doing it.

'So you're just going to go back and leave things as they are?' she said, realizing she was failing to convince her to stay.

'Could you just tell her that I said I'm sorry . . .'

At Kei's words Fumiko's expression turned suddenly grim. 'But that's . . . but I don't think you mean that. Do you regret giving birth to Miki? Can't you see that saying sorry can only mean that it was your mistake to have her?'

I haven't given birth to her yet. I haven't. But I have no second thoughts about my decision to do so.

On seeing Kei clearly shake her head in response, Fumiko said, 'Let me call Miki.'

Kei couldn't reply.

'I'll go and get her.'

Fumiko didn't wait for Kei to reply. She simply disappeared into the back room, well aware that time was of the essence.

'Hey, Fumiko,' said the man as he followed her into the back room.

Oh, what am I to do?

Left alone in the cafe, Kei stared at the coffee in front of her.

Fumiko is right. But that just seems to make it more difficult to know what to say.

Then Miki appeared; Fumiko had her hands on her shoulders.

Rather than at Kei, Miki's eyes were directed at the floor.

'Come on, sweetie, don't waste this moment,' Fumiko said.

Miki . . .

Kei meant to speak her name out loud, but no voice came.

'OK then,' Fumiko said, lifting her hands from Miki's shoulders. She looked quickly at Kei and then retreated to the back room.

Even after Fumiko had gone, Miki continued to look down at the floor in silence.

I'm going to have to say something . . .

Kei removed her hand from the cup and took a breath. 'So. Are you well?' she asked.

Miki lifted her head a little and looked at Kei. 'Yes,' she said in a quiet, tentative voice.

'You help out here?'

'Yeah.'

Miki's answers were blunt and monosyllabic. Kei was finding it difficult to continue talking.

'Both Nagare and Kazu are in Hokkaido?'

'Yeah.'

Miki continued to avoid looking at Kei's face. Each time she answered, she spoke a little more softly. There didn't seem to be much she wanted to talk about.

Without giving it much thought, Kei asked, 'Why did you stay here?'

Oops . . .

Kei regretted asking the question the moment it left her lips. When she realized that she hoped to hear Miki say that it was so she could meet her, she knew how insensitive such a forthright question must have sounded. She looked down in embarrassment.

But then Miki spoke. 'Well, you see,' she began in her soft voice, 'I make the coffee for the people in that seat.'

'Make the coffee?'

'Yeah, like Kazu always did.'

'Oh.'

'It's my job now.'

'Really?'

'Yeah.'

But there the flow of conversation abruptly ended. Miki didn't seem to know what else to say and turned her gaze downwards. Kei was unable to find any words to say next, but there was one thing she wanted to ask.

Bringing you into this world was the only thing that I did for you. Can you forgive me for that?

But how could she expect to receive such forgiveness? She had caused so much sadness.

Miki's reaction made Kei feel she had been selfish to come. Finding it increasingly difficult to look at her, Kei looked down at the coffee before her.

The surface of the coffee filling the cup was ever so slightly trembling. There was no longer any rising steam. Judging by the temperature of the cup, it would soon be time for her to leave.

What was it that I came here to do? Was there any point in my coming from the future? It all seems so pointless now. The only thing that has come from it is more suffering for Miki. When I return to the past, no matter how I try, it won't change Miki's unhappiness.

That cannot be changed. Take Kohtake, for instance, she returned to the past, but it didn't cure Fusagi. And likewise, Hirai wasn't able to stop her sister from dying.

Kohtake got to receive her letter, while Hirai met her sister. Fusagi's illness is still worsening and Hirai will never see her sister again.

It's the same for me as well. There is nothing I can do that will change the fifteen years that Miki has spent in sadness.

Although she had been granted her wish of visiting the future, she still felt utter despair.

'Well, I can't let the coffee go cold . . .' Kei said as she reached out and took the coffee cup.

Time to go back.

But at that moment she heard footsteps approaching. Miki had walked right up to her.

She put the cup back on the table and looked directly at her daughter.

Miki . . .

Kei didn't know what Miki was thinking. But she couldn't take her eyes away from her face. Miki was standing so close, she could touch her.

Miki took a deep breath. 'Just before . . .' she said with a trembling voice. 'When you said to Fumiko that I didn't want to meet . . . It's not like that.'

Kei listened, hanging on every word.

'I always thought that if we met, I would want to talk to you . . .'

There were so many things that Kei wanted to ask also.

'But when it actually happened, I didn't know what to say.'

Kei hadn't known what to say either. She dreaded how Miki

might be feeling. She'd failed to put the things she wanted to ask into words.

'And yes . . . there have been times when I have been sad.'

Kei could well imagine. The thought of Miki alone like that was heart-wrenching for her.

I cannot change those sad times of yours.

'But . . .' Miki smiled bashfully as she took a little step closer. 'I am really glad for the life you gave me.'

It takes courage to say what has to be said. It no doubt took Miki all of her courage to express her feelings to the mother she had just met. Her voice wavered with uncertainty, but it conveyed her true feelings.

But . . .

Large teardrops began flowing from Kei's eyes.

But giving birth to you is the only thing I will ever be able to do for you.

Miki also began crying. But using both hands to wipe away the tears, she smiled sweetly.

'Mum.' She said it in a nervous, excited voice but Kei heard it clearly.

Miki was calling her *Mum*.

But I haven't given you anything . . .

Kei covered her face with both hands. Her shoulders shuddered as she wept.

'Mum.'

Hearing her name called again, Kei suddenly remembered. It soon must be time to say goodbye.

'What?' Kei lifted up her face and smiled, reciprocating Miki's feelings.

'Thank you,' Miki said with the broadest of smiles. 'Thank

you for having me. Thank you . . .' She looked at Kei and quickly held up a peace sign.

'Miki.'

'Mum.'

At that moment, Kei's heart sang with happiness: she was the mother of this child. She wasn't just a parent – she was the mother of the girl standing before her. She was unable to stop the tears from gushing.

I finally understand.

The present didn't change for Kohtake, but she banned everyone from using her maiden name and changed her attitude towards Fusagi. She would be with Fusagi to continue being his wife, even though she had vanished from his memory. Hirai abandoned her successful bar to rejoin her family. While repairing her relationship with her parents, she was learning the traditional ways of the inn from square one.

The present doesn't change.

Nothing about Fusagi changed, but Kohtake came to enjoy her conversations with him. Hirai had still lost her sister, but the photo she sent to the cafe showed her looking happy with her parents.

The present hadn't changed – but those two people had. Both Kohtake and Hirai returned to the present with a changed heart.

Kei gently closed her eyes.

I was so absorbed in the things that I couldn't change, I forgot the most important thing.

Filling in for her, Fumiko had been by Miki's side for these fifteen years. Nagare had been there for Miki as her father, showering her with love, no doubt going some way to make up for her absence. Also filling in for her, Kazu had lavished Miki with kindness, playing the role of mother and big sister. She realized that there had been all these loving people around Miki, earnestly supporting her growth for the fifteen years she had been gone, wishing for her happiness.

Thank you for growing up so happily and healthily. Just by growing up so fit and well, you have made me so happy. That's all I want to say to you . . . this is how I feel deep down.

'Miki . . .' Leaving her flowing tears unwiped, Kei gave her best smile to Miki. 'Thank you, for the honour of having you.'

Upon Kei's return from the future, her face was a tearful mess. But it was immediately plain to everyone that these were not tears of sadness.

Nagare sighed in relief and Kohtake burst into tears.

But Kazu smiled with such kindness, it was as if she had seen what had happened for herself. 'Welcome home,' she said.

The next day, Kei checked into hospital. In spring, the next year, a healthy, happy baby girl came into this world.

The magazine piece on the urban legend had stated, '*At the end of the day, whether one returns to the past or travels to the future, the present does not change. So it raises the question: just what is the point of that chair?*'

But Kazu still goes on believing that, no matter what difficulties people face, they will always have the strength to overcome them. It just takes heart. And if the chair can change someone's heart, it clearly has its purpose.

But with her cool expression, she will just say, 'Drink the coffee before it gets cold.'

BEFORE THE COFFEE GETS COLD SERIES

More than 1 million copies sold worldwide

In a charming Tokyo cafe, customers are offered the unique experience of time-travel. But there are rules and the journey does not come without risks. Customers must return to the present before the coffee gets cold . . .

Translated from Japanese by Geoffrey Trousselot, Toshikazu Kawaguchi's heartwarming and wistful series tells the stories of people who must face up to their past in order to move on with their lives.

What would you do if you could travel back in time?